For my mom, for always believing in me.

And for my dad, who stepped up and never gave up on us, and for introducing us to new things.

And for my little sibling, for always inspiring me and being one of my best and closest friends.

And for my best friends, Sarah and Serenity, for always encouraging me.

I love you all <3

Table of Contents

Prologue

*H*igh winds churn the sea, dark clouds lining the night sky. Boats rock, bumping and crashing into each other and the docks, where they are moored. Waves crash violently against cliff sides; huge, sharp rocks jutting out of the sea close to the shores. A crack of thunder sounds, lightning flashing two seconds later, illuminating a terrifying manor.

A man and a woman run out of the front door of the manor. The man is holding a sword in one hand, his other hand on the woman's back, urging her forward. The woman is carrying a small boy, no older than six or seven years. The rain has turned the ground into mud. The woman slips on the mud in her rush, going down to one knee. The boy drops his stuffed rabbit as he's jostled around. The man helps them up and they continue forward.

The boy reaches out with one hand. He cries out: "Bunny! I lost Bunny!"

They stop. The man goes back for the stuffed toy, but a ghostly, floating hand snatches it up before he can grab it and takes it back to the manor. He stumbles back, fear striking him.

He urges his family to continue, yelling over the wind and rain. "I'm sorry, son! We must continue on! Our home is lost!"

They turn their back, the boy screaming as tears stream down his face. They don't get far before a loud, ghostly, maniacal laugh reaches their ears, echoing from the manor's open door.

…………….

The stuffed rabbit floats in the ghostly hand before being placed in a red hand. The man sighs, rubbing as much of the dirt off the toy as possible. He looks out the door, careful to not be seen at the family running from their home.

Another man, bigger in height and weight, comes up behind him, clapping his shoulder. "Well done, Leucious. They'll live another day yet."

He sighs again. How could he have allowed Chrom to talk him into this?

He looks at the other magic caster on the other side of the door. The hideous laughter outside calms down, being overtaken by the thunder. He looked scared when he spotted Chrom. Of course, he was only young, at least a decade younger than Leucious was. What could he have done that Chrom brought him along?

What was Chrom's plan?

Chapter 1

Gathering the Party

*I*t's an overcast day in the town of Kilmarnock. The streets are not busy, but the coming and going of the townsfolk from the shops flows steadily. Those that stand too close together part and regroup, presumably to let someone through.

Two women are talking to each other at an apple stand in a different part of the town.

"Did you hear about poor Missus Cliffbane?" The first townswoman asks.

"Aye, I did. Poor Missus Cliffbane, losin' her son so soon after her husband's death."

They continue their chatter, when a tall, red-headed woman approaches them. "Excuse me, ladies, sorry to interrupt you, but I must ask for your assistance."

"Get outta here, cretin! No one is going to be givin' you nothin'!"

The red-head smiles. "I can assure you, madame, that I am not looking nor asking for coin."

The first townswoman speaks up. "Then what do you want?" The women turn and look at her. "Hey, wait a minute! You ain't from 'round 'ere!"

Her smile only widens. "No, ma'am, I am not. I am an adventurer from several towns north of your quaint little town. Where could one such as me go to find adventure around here?"

The second townswoman looks at her questioningly. "You're an adventurer, and you don't know where to look?"

"Every place is different, is it not?"

Just as a remark was going to be made, the first townswoman places a hand on the second woman's shoulder, making her stay quiet. She regards the adventurer.

"The Iron Lamp Tavern's the only place round 'ere where you might find an adventure."

"Would you be so kind as to point me in the right direction of this tavern?"

……………..

A sign reading 'IRON LAMP TAVERN' hangs above a door. Sitting to the right of the door is a small figure, who seems to be wrapped in a hooded, black-feathered cloak. Dark eyes shine from under the hood as they watch the townsfolk, going about their daily lives, pass in front of them. He flips a silver coin over his fingers.

The tavern's door opens, and a man comes flying out. He is sprawled out on the ground before he's able to stagger back onto his feet, swaying a little. The door closes.

"Ah, fuck you! I'll take my business elsewhere! Maybe someplace where it's more appreciated!" His words are slurred. He soon notices the hooded figure. "What're you looking at?"

The hooded figure says nothing and continues to stare forward. The man huffs and walks up the street, away from the tavern. As he's walking, he notices a red-headed woman in leather armor and a pine green cloak walking towards him. He smirks. Just as they're about to pass each other, he grabs her by the shoulder.

"How's about you and I go back to my place, yeah? I'll show you a good time."

"How's about no." She mocks him. "I have no interest in you. Now, unhand me before you lose your hand."

"Look, lady, I'm offering you the best time of your li- "his scream cuts his sentence off as the bones in his hand snap.

The female adventurer pulls a dagger from inside her cloak, then holds it against his throat. "How much of a refusal do you need?" She releases his wrist and moves the dagger away from him. She kicks at his knee, and he drops to the ground, clutching his wrist. "I would see a healer, if I were you."

She walks away from him, and he falls forward, crying out in pain. She looks at the shops lining both sides of the street, watching their signs.

She spots the sign to the Iron Lamp Tavern. "Ah, there it is."

Her steps quicken slightly as she approaches the tavern. She then yelps as she falls forward, grunting as her hands splay out in front of her and her chin hits the ground. When she looks forward, she sees that she's only four feet away from the door.

"Ow…"

A cawing laugh comes from close by. She looks up as she props her hands under her body, preparing to get up. She finds the source of the laugh, to see the hooded figure clutching his stomach in laughter.

"Oh, that was priceless! Best show I've ever seen!" He says in between his laughs.

"It's not funny." She says begrudgingly. She picks herself up and approaches the laughing figure, staying four feet away from him.

"Oh, but it is! First, you beat that guy up, only to then trip over a rock!" His laughter calms before stopping. He caws as he looks at her. "You wouldn't happen to be going into the tavern?"

"I am. Why do you ask?" She asks, dusting herself off.

"I was waiting for somebody to go in with." He hops up from his seat before going to the door. She takes note that he is about half her height. He looks back at her. "Well? What are you waiting for? An invitation?

....

The jovial chords of a lute play in the tavern. Everyone inside is either sitting down and having a drink with their party or are gambling away their hard-earned gold. The door opens, the hooded figure hopping in, the red-headed adventurer closing the door behind them. The cloaked figure hops onto a barstool with the other adventurer sitting beside him.

"Ah, I know what yer kind like." He remarks, before looking over at the woman. "What'll it be, miss?"

The hooded figure answers before she's able to. "The best for my friend, good sir!"

"Alright. One Avishum Special and one Home Special!" He yells behind him. "Anything to drink?"

"A water for my feathery acquaintance." The Avishum is visibly disappointed. "As for me, surprise me."

"Ah, a lady that's not scared of a good drink. I'll be back with yer drinks."

The bartender walks off. The Avishum leans against the bar, regarding his friend with the best pouty look that he can muster.

"That's a boring drink choice."

"Don't order for me, and I won't order for you."

He props his head up with one hand and grumbles out: "You're no fun."

The bartender returns with their drinks. "Here you go. Water for the Avishum and a blueberry honey ale for the lady."

They take their drinks. "Thank you. How much do I owe you?"

The bartender holds up his hand. "No cost. First time patron's meals and drinks are free."

The Avishum's mood brightens up. "Wow, really? That's incredible!"

"So, what brings you to town? We don't see much of your likes 'round 'ere."

"Well, I am- "

The female adventurer doesn't get a chance to finish her sentence as the door opens. Every patron stops their conversations, and the lute goes quiet. Four males in City Watch attire are standing around the door, and a shorter female stands in the middle, her brown hair pulled back into a tight bun. She scans the room.

She addresses the room. "Who amongst you has just assaulted a man outside of this dwelling?"

Confused looks pass among the room. There is unintelligible murmuring. The red-head leans over to the Avishum and whispers. "Do you think she's talking about the guy whose wrist I broke?"

He speaks in a normal tone. "I don't know. She might be."

The adventurer winces from how loud her acquaintance was in the quiet atmosphere. A pair of eyes land on the two of them.

"You, there. What is the Avishum talking about?"

She mutters to the bird. "Whisper next time!" She then gives her attention to the guards, leaning against the bar. "I broke a man's wrist about thirty feet away from this establishment."

The guard narrows her eyes. "I would like to speak to the both of you. Outside."

The Avishum whines. "But we just ordered food! We're waiting for it now!"

"Outside. Now."

"Might I make a suggestion?" Inquires the red-head.

....

The three of them sit around a table as they wait for the food. The female guard sits across from the other two. The rest of the guards surround the table.

"Why did you assault that man?"

"How do we know that it's the same man?"

The guard's eye twitches. "He has a broken wrist. When we were questioning him earlier, he mentioned that a fair-skinned, red-headed woman with pointy ears went crazy on him and broke his wrist. Does any of this sound familiar?"

She snickers. "I think we both know that there were other choice words to what he said. But yes, I did break his wrist. In an act of self-defence."

"Why do you claim self-defence?"

The other adventurer piped up as he picked up his drink. "He was drunk when he left here." He sticks his beak into his mug.

The guard raises an eyebrow.

"The bird is right. He staggered his way towards me and grabbed my arm. He made a provocative suggestion. I warned him that he should remove his hand." She sits with an heir of confidence as she crosses one leg over the other, grabbing her drink. "I gave him a chance. And he made the wrong choice. I believe that my actions may have sobered him up.

The guard sighs. "He is known for the actions that you have stated. I don't expect any lesser action from a rogue." She stands. "I believe that we are done here. Thank you for your time."

The mug meets the table forcefully. "I have more dignity than that. I am a paladin, not a rogue, my lady."

"A paladin? Then why do you dress as a rogue?"

"It is more comfortable. And more flexible."

The guard regards the paladin before looking at the other members of the Watch.

"Head back. There's nothing more that can be done here." They nod before walking out of the tavern. "Torren! Ale and a House Special!" She calls out before sitting back down.

"Right away, miss Stoutbrow." Torren, the bartender, responds.

Water bubbles sputter from the Avishum's mug. He takes his beak out of his mug, water dripping into his lap.

"You're a Stoutbrow?"

"You've heard of my family?"

"No. It just sounds like an important name."

He returns his beak to his mug. The two women sitting with him give him an incredulous look. The pointy eared woman shakes her head before she takes a drink. A waitress approaches the table, tray in hand.

"Here we are. One Avishum Special and one House Special." She says, placing the food in front of them. "Yer ale. And yer food will be done soon, miss Stoutbrow."

The Stoutbrow woman takes a drink as the waitress walks off, then sets her mug down. "Well, you know my last name. I am Serena. You might recognize my family name because my father is the head of the Watch. I am in my first year of work with them, having started this last Spring when I celebrated my twentieth year. What about you two?"

The Avishum jumps in his seat in excitement. "I'm Three!" He states before digging into his food. His tablemates give him a questioning look.

"And your name?" Asks the other woman.

The broth from his fish chowder drips from his beak as he looks at them. "Three."

"No, your name, not your age." Serena clarifies.

"Three."

"I think he's saying that it's both. Stop me if I'm wrong, but last year, you would have been two years old?" Three nods, food still falling from his beak. "So, your name was 'Two'?"

Three caws excitedly. "Yes, that's right! I'm a rogue pirate who is without a crew or ship."

"Calm now, Three, we're in a public setting." The paladin takes another drink. "I guess that leaves me. I am Valindra Theharice. I am an elven paladin, four-hundred-and-fifty years old, and for the last four-hundred years, I have been fighting dragons."

"Wow, you're old!" Three exclaims.

Valindra's eye twitches.

"An elven paladin? That fights dragons?" Serena looks at her suspiciously, her food being placed in front of her. "Why did you stop?"

"I decided that a change of scene was necessary." She picks up a forkful of her food, her chicken nearly falling from it. "So, I left my homeland while the times have been calm and thought that I would try adventuring."

The waitress reappears at their table. "An adventurer, you say. Have you heard of Cliffbane Manor?"

"I recall hearing some townsfolk talking about a Cliffbane earlier today. Tell me, would they be the same family that owns the manor? What is their story?"

Serena swallows down a mouthful of potato. "You know that is a matter for the Watch, Lydia."

"Of course, miss." Lydia, the waitress, walks away.

Food flings from Three's beak as he calls after her. "Hey! Come back! You can't tell us something interesting and then walk off!"

"It is my work to deal with. I can only hope that I can solve it and earn a little more respect from my commanding officer."

The last part of Serena's sentence fades off, almost inaudible. Not a word is missed by Valindra, though. The three of them sit in silence as they eat and drink. Serena's face is long in lost hope. Three and Valindra look at each other, seeming to come to a silent agreement.

"You know, we could be of service to you." Serena looks at Valindra. "So, may you fill us in?"

Serena smiles. These adventurers could prove useful to her. She happily agrees to fill them in.

Three speaks up before she gets a chance to, though. "Hey, can I call you 'Val'?"

Chapter 2

On the Road

The waning crescent moon does little to help guide the young boy, no older than twelve or thirteen, as he sneaks up to a large barn. He creeps along the wall, careful where he steps. He reaches the door, checking his surroundings, before opening the barn door and walking in, careful that the sword at his hip, being too big for him, doesn't hit or scrape against anything.

He walks back out a few seconds later, leading a horse without a saddle. He guides her to a tree stump, stepping onto it and mounting her. He clicks his tongue, and the mare walks off. As soon as they get further away from the town, he clicks his tongue two more times, and the mare takes off in a trot. After two more clicks, she goes into a canter, and he steers her up the road, taking off into the night.

.,……………..

The sun beats down on the town. There's a loud raucous coming from the tavern. It gets louder as the door opens, Serena walking out, followed by Three and Valindra. Just before she closes the door, Valindra looks back at the tavern.

"Thank you for your service, Torren. I'll be sure to return!" She does not know if he heard her or not.

She catches up with Three and Serena, the door closing behind her as she walks off. Serena is mounting her horse, issued to her by the Watch. Valindra approaches them, slowing her walk to a stop.

"What's the plan?" She asks them.

"I'm heading back to headquarters and gathering the rest of the information pertaining to the Cliffbane Manor case. I'll meet up with you two in an hour outside of their current abode." She points a finger at both. "And don't be late."

"Same to you."

Serena takes her reins in either hand, guiding her horse in the right direction, taking off in a trot. As soon as she takes off, Valindra turns and walks in the opposite direction. Three, not knowing what else to do, follows her.

"Where are we going, Val?" He asks once he's caught up to her. "The Cliffbane's live in the south-west direction."

"We'll be needing horses. I recall seeing a stable when I walked this way earlier."

"Oh, gee, Val, do you really think we need horses? What if we can't afford them?" He caws, trying to catch up with her long steps.

She stops abruptly, Three almost running into her back. She turns and looks down at him, her face showing annoyance.

"As I told you in the tavern, it's 'Valindra', not 'Val'. As for the horses, we can possibly bargain for a better price. Besides, we need a way to travel to the manor. Unlike you, I don't have wings, so I can't fly there."

She stalks off. Three runs after her, ending up beside her as he follows her. He stays quiet, somehow figuring that it's best not to say anything after annoying her. Soon enough, they find the stables.

The sound of the horse's hooves can be heard clomping around their stalls, paired with other various horse noises. The stable operator is close by, leading another horse to its stall. Valindra and Three approach him. He doesn't appear to be very happy.

"We're looking for horses." Three tells him, getting straight to the point.

"What was that?" He questions, clearly not in the mood to be helpful or be annoyed by those who don't know their manners.

Valindra intervenes before Three can make anything worse. "Sorry about him, he apparently doesn't know his manners. This is Three, and I am Valindra. We are looking for a means of travel."

"The name's Cain. If you're looking for a horse, it's five gold for every horse, plus extra for every day they're gone. And they must be returned. I'm already short a mare." He grumbles the last part angrily.

Three slumps forward, disappointed. Valindra has a questioning look about her face, tilting her head slightly to the left.

"What happened to your mare?"

"Someone stole away with her yestereve."

Valindra taps a finger to her chin, thinking. "What would be the cost if we only hired one horse? Big enough for me and my companion?"

Cain takes a moment to think. "Three gold up front, two silver per day."

Three turns his head, his eyes lighting up as he sees something. He walks in the direction of the object. Valindra notices that he's walking away but says nothing. She continues to barter with Cain.

"What if we were to bring back your mare?"

Cain takes this into consideration, rethinking his price. "Two gold instead of three upfront."

"I'll take your best, fastest, and strongest stallion, then."

Cain goes into the stable. While he's gone, Valindra searches the grounds for Three. She finds him around back, trying to pocket a horseshoe.

"Now, Three, we aren't thieves. Put the horseshoe down."

"But, shiny." He caws.

"Put it down. Before we lose our bargain."

"What's goin' on 'ere?"

She turns around as Three looks behind her. Cain approaches them.

"Sorry about him. He found a loose horseshoe." She apologizes.

Three holds it up and gives a low caw. "Shiny."

"That ole thing? Keep it."

Three perks up excitedly. "Really?"

"Yeah, I was goin' to have it melted down anyway. Now come on, your horse is ready." Cain beckons them to follow him.

They round the corner to the front of the stables. Standing there, ready for travel, was a rust-colored Belgian stallion with white around his hooves. While Three hops up to the stallion, Valindra loosens her coin purse from her belt. She rummages around in it before handing Cain two gold coins.

"The rest upon return." She returns her purse to her belt, asking Cain: "What is the name of this glorious beast?"

Cain pockets the gold. "Cider's the name. How long do you think you'll be needin' him?"

Valindra leads Cider over to a box. She helps Three mount him before sitting behind him with ease. "A week at the longest, I think. I do hope, however, that this takes no longer than two days."

"Just remember that my horse is to be returned. And remember your promise to find my missing mare."

"I shall remember." She notices Three putting the horseshoe into his travel bag. "Have you thanked him yet, Three?"

"Oh!" Three looks at Cain. "Thanks for the shiny, sir!"

"Yer welcome. Safe travels, adventurers. And Godspeed."

"It was a pleasure doing business with you." Valindra steers Cider's reins and lightly kicks at his sides, taking off in a walk.

. . . .

The afternoon sun is hot, the wind thankfully keeping Serena cool. She's waiting by a fence, her brown Percheron tied to it. She looks to the main road, growing impatient.

"Where are those two? I told them not to be late." She says to herself.

She hears hooves. She looks to her left and sees Valindra slowing a horse from a gallop to a canter as they turn up the driveway, slowing down more the closer they get to the fence. She brings Cider to a stop when she reaches Serena. She dismounts and leads Cider to the fence, tying him beside Serena's horse before helping Three down.

"You were almost late. Another minute, and I would have started without you."

"Sorry, it took longer to bargain with Cain than I thought it would." She pets Cider.

"The stable operator?" Serena stands straighter, no longer leaning against the fence as Valindra opens the fence gate and walks through, following behind Three. "He's usually easy to bargain with."

They make their way up to the house. "Someone stole his mare. To say he is not pleased is an understatement. I promised to bring her back home." Valindra informs her, noting Serena's look of surprise. She knocks on the door. "Misses Cliffbane? Are you home?"

There is no answer. Serena knocks on the wooden door once more. "Misses Cliffbane?"

"Go away. I don't want company." The voice through to door sounded upset.

"Misses Cliffbane, my name is Serena. I'm from the Watch. My associates and I are here to help you."

There is more silence behind the door. Serena and Valindra look at each other, both wondering if they would be able to get inside. Three hops from one foot to the other, getting rather impatient waiting there. They hear the lock turn, and the door cracks open slightly. Half of misses Cliffbane's face shows, but it's enough to see that she's been crying.

"I didn't ask for any help. How can I trust you?"

Valindra clamps Three's beak shut. "Good afternoon, ma'am. My friend Serena is a member of the city guard. My feathery friend and I are adventuring friends of hers who offered our services to help your family."

"Can you help my son?" She sniffles.

Valindra gives her a friendly smile, turning her charm up a notch. "May we come inside to talk?"

Misses Cliffbane stands there for a moment, looking at all three of them. She considers them for a moment, then stands behind the door, opening it the rest of the way. She beckons them in.

Charming person, isn't she? Serena thinks to herself. *I'll have to remember that.*

They all walk in, Valindra letting Three and Serena go in ahead of her. Misses Cliffbane closes the door, then leads them further into her house. It's a small space, with stairs leading to the upstairs. The three adventurer's follow behind the upset widow into the kitchen, where she pulls a hot kettle off the woodstove.

"I was making some tea." She sniffles again. "Would anyone else like some tea?"

Valindra gives her a wide smile. "We would love to have some tea, Misses Cliffbane. Let me help you prepare it."

Very charming. Could get us into trouble. Serena thinks, but accepts the invitation for tea.

……………..

Serena and Three sit at a small wooden table with Misses Cliffbane, wooden cups of tea sitting in front of them. Misses Cliffbane holds her cup in between her hands. Valindra stands at a nearby window, holding her tea and looking out the window towards the north. A somber look passes her face. She looks as if she's missing something…

Serena breaks the silence. "I understand the loss of family, Misses Cliffbane, but we need to know what happened. To your family, and your home."

Misses Cliffbane sniffles, looking down at her tea. "Six years ago, my family and I were driven from our home. We were sitting by the warmth from the fireplace, when objects started flying about, voices telling us to leave. Almost as if the place had become haunted. My son, on our way out, had dropped his stuffed rabbit. My husband went to retrieve it, and a hand appeared out of nowhere, taking it back into the manor. There was this horrifying laugh. None of us ever went back."

Serena places her hand on her forearm in comfort. "What of your husband? I've heard that he passed recently."

"He was attacked by a wolf while he was hunting last winter."

"And your son?" Valindra asked, taking a sip of her tea, coming back to her current surroundings.

"I haven't seen him since he went to bed. I started looking for him as soon as I noticed that he was missing, but I haven't been able to find him."

"He probably went back to the manor."

Misses Cliffbane looks at Valindra. "Why would he do that now? It's been six years."

"How far away is the manor, Misses Cliffbane?" Serena asks, trying to bring the attention back to the case.

She tells them that the manor is about six hours away by horse. They thank her for the information and finish their teas. Valindra is the first to run out of the house, followed by Serena. They head towards the horses. Three stays behind for a moment and stands on the porch with Misses Cliffbane.

"Thank you for the tea. And sorry about your husband." He has a determined look on his face. "We will bring your son home. Don't you worry about that."

Serena and Valindra have already untied their horses and have mounted them. Valindra looks back to the house and calls out to Three.

"Three! We must be on our way!"

Three nods to Misses Cliffbane before hopping off the porch. He unfurls his wings and flies off, following behind his friends. They've set off to the manor in a gallop. They follow the road to town, but turn down the path into the forest, Cider and Valindra leading the party.

Once they get further up the road and farther from civilisation, they slow the horses down to a trot. Three flies down low enough so that he's able to land and sit behind Valindra. Serena moves up beside them, then slows her trot to match pace with Valindra.

"What are you thinking? Why did you run out like that?" Serena asks Valindra.

"I'm thinking that the Cliffbane child is getting himself into more trouble than he realizes."

"What do you mean, Val?" Three asks.

"You've heard the rumours of Cliffbane Manor being haunted, yes? What Misses Cliffbane described verifies those rumours. I think that there's something else going on, though; that they were purposefully driven away."

Three is confused.

"Care to explain so that we're all on the same page?" Serena asks her.

"I don't have an explanation for why their belongings were flying around. But the hand that appeared out of nowhere? And the ghostly laughter? All sounds like witchcraft to me."

"Like Mage Hand and Thaumaturgy?"

Valindra looks at Serena, quirking an eyebrow. "Exactly like Mage Hand and Thaumaturgy. How do you know so much, for someone so young and part of the guard?"

Serena blushes. "I studied a lot of different material before I became a member of the Watch. I figured that it would come in handy."

Valindra smirks. "A bookworm? How handy."

Serena looks away, her blush darkening.

They travel a few more miles, red, yellow, orange, and some green leaves falling around them. They hear a horse whinny ahead of them.

Serena reaches to brandish her longsword, but Valindra holds out her hand to stop her. They trot further up the road and find a black Percheron.

"What's a horse doing out here?" Three speaks up.

"My god. That's Cain's mare!" Serena exclaims.

"That means that the Cliffbane boy did not tie her up." Valindra remarks. "We need to hurry and get to the Manor as soon as possible."

She brings Cider to a halt, Serena bringing her horse to a stop as well. Valindra dismounts and searches through her bag on Cider's side. She pulls a length of rope from her pack. She walks towards the mare, approaching calmly. The horse allows her to pet her snout, and Valindra is able to tie the rope around her neck.

"What are you doing, Val?" Three asks from Cider's back.

"And what do you mean 'as soon as possible'?" Serena asks.

Valindra brings the mare closer to the party. "I am not leaving Cain's horse here. And I mean that we need to move, and quickly. Three, are you able to ride her?"

"Sure can, Val."

Valindra brings the horse up to beside Cider. She helps Three down from her horse before boosting him onto the mare's back. Serena rides ahead of them and turns her horse around, stopping in the middle of the road.

"We cannot ride any further tonight. We must make camp."

Valindra mounts Cider. "Are you afraid of what's in the dark? Don't tell me that you're not able to see them." She chuckles. Serena doesn't answer her. "Oh, for the – Three, can you see in the dark?"

"Oh, no can do on that, Val."

"Oh, for the love of the Gods!" She looks towards the sky. "Sif, please grant me the strength to get through this night." She lowers her head again and pinches the bridge of her nose. "Do you both have rope?"

They nod.

"Good. Tie one end around yourselves. We'll attach the other ends to me."

Three happily gathers the rope from his pack and starts following Valindra's orders. Serena, on the other hand, does not.

"I don't think that that's a good id- "

"There is a young boy in danger." Valindra grabs the untied end of the rope from Three and ties herself to him. "If anything happens to him, it's on your head."

"I still don't think- "

"Then don't think. Brandish your rope. We'll rest when we get there. We ride tonight."

…………….

The room around him is dark, darker than he's ever seen before. The Cliffbane boy is barely able to see the rope tied around him, keeping him from going anywhere. He can't tell if there's anyone else in the room. He starts to shake, afraid of being alone in the dark. He starts to cry.

"Hey, don't cry." A deep voice calls out to him. "You're not alone."

Chapter 3

The Garden

*V*alindra and Cider lead the party down the darkened road,
crunching leaves, kicking small pebbles, snapping twigs. The manor soon
appears behind the line of trees, looming over them, giving off a
foreboding gloom. She brings Cider to a halt, her party's horses stopping
just behind her.

"Here we are." She sighs. "Cliffbane Manor."

"Even scarier in person." Three shivers, his feathers ruffling.

"So, what do we do now?" Serena asks.

Valindra notices Three yawn out the corner of her eye. "We untie
ourselves and dismount. You two light a couple torches. I'll tie down the
horses."

They untie the knots and dismount. Three rummages around in his
pack, looking for a flint and steel while Serena produces the torches. They
work together to light them, sparks flying before one finally ignites.
Valindra approaches them and helps them light the second torch.

"How are the horses?" Serena asks.

"Tired. I tied them close enough to a tall patch of grass so that they can eat. They will be needing water, though."

"We need water, too!" Three states, yawning once again.

"We'll have to use our rations."

"Save your rations." Valindra receives tired, questioning looks from her party. "I think I passed by a garden on my way to you two."

"There wouldn't have been anyone to tend to it since the Cliffbane's were run out."

"It is still worth trying. We could probably find a water trough, too."

With Three and Serena carrying the torches, they walk back in the direction that Valindra came from, following the stone wall to their right. They follow it until they reach a gate. Serena tries to open it, to no avail.

"It's locked. We can't get in to look around."

"I can help with this!" Three goes up to the lock, then looks at Valindra. "Hey, Val? Can you hold my torch?"

Once Valindra takes his torch, Three takes off his pack and looks through it, pulling out his thieves' tools. He sets to work on the lock.

"I am working with a criminal. That's going to go over well with the Watch." Serena complains.

"I'm a rogue, not a criminal. And if I were a criminal," the lock clicks and turns. He removes his tools and pushes the gates open, "then this 'criminal' declares this garden open!"

Three returns his tools to his bag. He takes his torch back from Valindra before walking into the garden. Sharing a glance with each other, Valindra shrugs and gestures for Serena to go ahead of her. Serena walks in, Valindra close behind. They notice right away that Three almost disappears in the tall grass. Valindra spots a well near the middle of the garden.

"Spread out, but not too thin. Try to look for any root vegetables. And be careful; we don't know what's hiding in the grass. I'm going to see if there's any water in the well."

Valindra moves towards the well. Serena and Three pair up before they start searching the garden. Valindra searches the ground as she makes her way over, careful of where she steps.

She spots a sizeable rock on the ground and crouches to pick it up. But before she can pick it up, she hears the grass to her right moving. There is no wind.

"Serena! Three! Stop moving!"

They stand up at her warning, about five feet apart. They stand completely still. Then Serena hears it.

"There's something in the grass."

Just as Serena says that, a weasel jumps out at Valindra. She manages to catch it but falls to her side in the process. Seeing Valindra go down, Serena brandishes her longsword.

"What happened? Where's Val?" Three asks, worry lacing his now-awakened voice.

"If you have a sword, brandish it and follow me."

Three draws his rapier. A weasel goes flying from where Valindra went down. She scrambles to her feet, drawing her own rapier in the process.

She yells. "Weasels!"

Serena looks around her, hearing the grass rustling around her. She finds the patch of moving grass, and quickly strikes. There is a shriek; she hit one! She brings her sword back, and the movement from the grass stops.

"Thankfully, I was faster than that one. Do we know how many there are?"

Valindra looks around, counting in her head. *One... two... three... five.*

"There's five left!" She calls out. Then yells: "Three! Behind you!"

Three starts to turn, but he's too late to dodge as the weasel sinks its teeth into his leg. He cries out. He pierces the weasel with his rapier.

"Three! Are you alright?" Valindra's voice held an obvious note of worry.

The weasel stops thrashing. Three grunts as he removes his sword from the weasel. "I'm fine!"

Serena gives a sharp cry as another weasel bites her leg. Valindra attempts to make her way towards them but ends up sidestepping the two weasels that attempt to bite her. She rebukes by piercing one with her rapier, killing it instantly.

"That's half of them. Be on your guard!"

Three grunts, another weasel biting his other leg. Serena kicks her leg, effectively removing the weasel that attacked her. The weasel lands with a thud and shakes its head before facing her again.

"That pinched quite a bit!" She remarks through gritted teeth.

Three thrusts his rapier into the weasel that just bit his leg, killing it. Valindra moves to sidestep the other weasel in front of her, but it moves before her, biting her. She grunts, grinding her teeth together. The one that Serena kicked off her shakes its head again. Valindra kills the one that just bit her, while Serena delivers the killing blow to the one that she dazed.

Serena's breathing is heavy. "Is everyone okay?"

"I've been better. But I can carry on." Three pants.

"Can you two make your way to me? I think that we should stick together from now on. My main objective is getting water for our horses."

They limp their way over to Valindra. Just as she crouches down again to pick up the rock from earlier, Three falls into her arms. She catches him, rock in hand.

"Are you sure that you're alright?" Valindra is quite concerned about her little friend.

"I am. Just small bites to my legs."

"How about you lean against me as we walk? If we get into any more trouble tonight, you take to the sky." Three nods, understanding. Valindra looks up at Serena. "Do you also require assistance?"

Serena shakes her head. "I'll be fine. It was only one bite."

Valindra nods, before turning to walk the rest of the way to the well, Three limping in step with her. Serena follows closely behind.

They stand together at the well. It is too tall for Three to see over the edge. Valindra motions for silence before she drops the rock into the well. The party waits, hearing nothing. Valindra and Serena both look down towards the bottom.

"What do your elven eyes see, Valindra?"

"There is water about a hundred feet down." She grabs the rope that hangs down from the cover and pulls on it, testing it. "The rope is steady enough. I'll pull the bucket up before we gather water."

She makes sure that Three is steadied against the well wall before she turns the lever. A questioning look crosses her face as she starts to turn it, then stops abruptly.

"What is it?" Serena asks.

"Take Three's torch and attach both to the well. Three, take to the sky. And Serena," Serena looks at her, already taking the torch from Three, "ready your shield."

Three takes to the sky as soon as Serena takes the torch from him. She attaches both to the well, then readies her shield. Three readies his short bow from above. Once they've gotten into position, Valindra raises the bucket some more. A poisonous snake strikes at Serena as soon as the bucket is almost to the brim of the well, but it bounces off her shield. Three lets an arrow fly, and it lands just shy of Serena's foot.

"Damn." Three mutters.

Ignoring the arrow by her foot, Serena swings her longsword over her head and brings it down, cleaving the snakes head in two. The snake falls limply, landing between Serena and the well.

With the snake now dead, Valindra raises the bucket the rest of the way. "That has to have been the fastest battle I have ever witnessed."

Three flies down and snatches the bucket away from Valindra as it emerges. He picks up his arrow as he lands, then inspects the inside of the bucket by the light of the torches.

He caws in excitement. "Silver! There's silver at the bottom of the bucket!"

"How much silver?" Serena asks, sheathing her sword.

"One, two… twelve. Twelve pieces, and no holes at the bottom."

Valindra looks around, then spots a shed in a corner of the garden.

"We'll split the silver later. There's a shed, about fifty feet that way." She points towards the south-east. "Serena, why don't you search for some vegetables. We might be able to make a stew out of the weasel meat. We should also search more of the area, look out for more enemies. If there aren't any, then we'll bring the horses in here."

"What would I use to gather the vegetables? The ground's as hard as a rock." She kicks the ground with the toe of her boot to prove her point.

"Use this." Valindra's cloak lifts only a little as she removes her dagger from its place at her hip.

Serena takes Valindra's dagger from her before taking one of the torches. She goes back to the corner of the garden that she was investigating. Three places his loosened arrow back into his quiver, pockets the silver, and walks towards Valindra, grabbing the other torch on his way by. They head towards the shed. As Serena digs for vegetables, Three picks the lock on the shed and, with Valindra's help, pries the door open. She leaves the torch with Three and leaves, passing by Serena as she gathers the horses. When she returns, horses in tow, Three had gotten a fire started and was stirring a pot of weasel meat while Serena peeled and cut up the vegetables.

Once she was sure that the horses were safe to roam, Valindra returned to her friends, sitting to the left of Three, being careful of how her cloak sits around her.

Once the stew was done, Valindra took their bowls and served them all. They all ate in silence, the crackle of the fire and the horses being the only source of noise around them. Three tipped his bowl, slurping loudly as he consumed the broth at the bottom of his bowl. The women looked at him; Serena looking almost disgusted, and Valindra with a look of discontent.

"Gods, I hope you don't always eat like that." Valindra says, her tone showing her discontent. Three wipes away the broth dripping from his beak with his arm.

"I'll take first watch tonight." Serena spoke up, breaking the awkward silence that followed. "You two should sleep."

"Are you sure? Do you want me to heal you before we sleep?" Valindra asked her.

"With your Lay on Hands? Save it. We might need it for later."

Valindra rests her arm on her knee, steadying her bowl. She raises an eyebrow in a questioning manner. "How do you know so much about paladins? Other than, of course, through study."

Serena lowers her spoon before placing her bowl on the ground beside her. She lowers her eyes in sorrow. "My brother." She was hesitant. "He… he _was_ a paladin."

Valindra lowers her own bowl, nodding once in understanding. "I'm sorry about your brother. Considering that, we are about to rest. And I would feel better if we were all at full health when we take watch."

Before Serena could protest, Three intervenes, handing her bowl back to her. "Eat up. Can't let good stew go to waste."

Given his gentle tone, Serena decides that she will take her bowl back and continue eating. She is surprised to see it filled nearly to the brim and gives a small smile, before it quickly vanishes. Three holds out a hand to Valindra, gesturing for her to give him her bowl.

"No thank you, Three. One is enough for me."

Three shrugs. "Suit yourself, Val." He dishes up some more stew for himself before sitting down. "So, how does this special healing thingy of yours work?" He brings the spoon up to his beak.

"I heal you by touch."

"Handy." Three chuckles as he brings another spoonful up to his beak and slurps it. "I could use some healing."

"I might be able to heal both of you. I can't heal much, but it should help. We're lucky that Serena took care of the snake so quickly, otherwise there would be more injuries."

"I'm sure a bite or two wouldn't have hurt us that much." Serena mutters under her breath, her spoon at her mouth.

Valindra looks at her, her spoon halfway to her mouth before she lowers it again. "I assure you that if that poisonous snake had bitten any of us, we would need more than the healing that I can manage."

"I-I knew that." Serena stammers, flustered.

"I'm sure you did. And don't be alarmed, but I put the snake in the corner of the shed."

Serena and Three give her an incredulous look before they exclaim, simultaneously: "Why would you do that?"

"This way, it can't poison our water supply, nor will the horses come across it. Besides, I threw it into a burlap sack, so we'll know where it is."

Serena shakes her head in disbelief before going back to eating. Three takes the spoon out of his mouth before he tips his head and bowl back, once again slurping the rest of his stew. Valindra gives him a look of disgust.

"You always eat like that, don't you?" She asks facetiously.

Three doesn't seem to hear her. He sets the bowl down. There is not a drop in the bowl. He wipes around his beak.

"I'll take the second watch."

"Then I'll take the last watch." Valindra also sets her bowl down. "I only need to rest for four hours, which gives both of you six hours of rest."

"Why do you only need four hours of sleep? That's unfair!" Three whines.

"She's a High Elf, Three. Those of the elven race have this ability where, when they rest for four hours, it's the same as having rested for eight hours."

"Really? Cool."

A corner of Valindra's mouth lifts in a smirk. She speaks under her breath: "Yeah, High Elf. We'll go with that." Three heard her that time, giving her a glance out of the side of his eyes.

She speaks up. "I sincerely hope that your knowledge on every other topic outweighs your knowledge of the elven race, Miss Stoutbrow."

Serena tilts her head, her eyes squinting in question. Valindra, from her seated position, turns and kneels towards Three. Three looks at her. She closes her forest green eyes, before tilting her head back. Her arms lift above her head, palms outstretched towards the sky.

She opens her eyes, a soft yellow-white glow emanating from them. The same glow surrounds her hands. She looks back down, bringing her arms back to her torso before she reaches for Three's legs. Her hands glow brighter as Three gives out a cawing laugh.

"That tickles!" He exclaims through his laughter.

The glow dies down a bit before Valindra removes her hands from his legs. The wounds that Three had were now gone, completely healed by her touch. Three inspects his legs in awe as Valindra gets up and moves toward Serena. The yellow-white glow almost seems to engulf her figure as she moves toward her, focusing the glow into her hands again as she kneels in front of Serena, the same glow surrounding Serena's lower legs.

A warm feeling passes through Serena from where Valindra heals her. Closing her eyes, she embraces the warmth as memories pass by her eyes. When she opens them again, she sees a brown-haired figure kneeling, healing her instead of Valindra. She gasps, but the figure disappears, Valindra's fire-red hair returning. Valindra removes her hands, the glow fading to nothing in her hands, travelling up her arms until finally disappearing from her eyes. She is concerned as to Serena's reaction. Tears come to Serena's eyes before she turns her head away.

"Three, why don't you get some rest first? You've had a long day."

"Okay, Val." He didn't need her to tell him twice. He stands and heads towards the shed. "Good night!"

Three disappears into the shed, not waiting for a response from either woman. Valindra sits beside Serena. There is silence between the two of them. Serena wipes a stray tear, sniffling as she does so.

"Are you alright?" Valindra finally asks her.

"I… I'm fine. Don't worry about me."

Valindra remains quiet a moment longer. When she speaks again, her voice is laced with concern. "Your brother must have healed you a lot, didn't he?"

Serena nods stiffly.

"I must have reminded you of him when I healed you, yes?"

Serena nods again, wiping more tears from her face. Her voice cracks. "I would run after him, wanting to follow him on his adventures. I would always trip over something; a rock, a stick, my own feet, you name it. If it was between him and I, there was a guarantee that I would find it. Anyway, I would trip and skin my knees. I would start crying because it stung so much from the dirt. But my brother would always turn back around and make sure that I was okay, healing me so that my father wouldn't see that I tried to follow after him again."

"Your brother sounds like he was a good man."

"He was. I wish I knew what happened to him."

Valindra places a hand on Serena's knee. The other woman looks at her. "You don't have to tell me about this if you don't want to. After all, we've only just met. When you feel like you want to talk, I'll be waiting for you."

"Thank you, Valindra."

"There is no need for thanks. Are you sure that you are good to take first watch? We can change shifts, if you'd like."

"No, I'll be fine." She dries her eyes with the heels of her palms. "Go, rest. I've got it."

"Only if you're sure." Valindra stands. "If anything should happen, you wake us up."

"Understood." She watches Valindra walk toward the shed.

When Valindra walks into the shed, she spots Three curled up on the floor, his wings acting as a makeshift blanket. She sits against the wall, close to him. She lifts her cloak a little, placing it over him. Three moves closer to her, cuddling up to her leg, sighing as he does. A small smile crosses Valindra's face. She wraps the rest of her cloak around her as best as she could before resting her head against the wall, soon drifting off to sleep.

....

Three shakes Valindra, attempting to wake her.

"Val?" He whisper-caws. "Val, wake up. It's your turn to go on watch."

Continuing to gently shake her, Three keeps calling to her, trying not to wake Serena on the other side of the shed. Valindra squeezes her eyes some more before they slowly open, only to be welcomed with Three's face right in front of hers. Three hops back as she stretches her arms above her head. She stands as Three lays down, this time beside Serena, resting the same way that Valindra was.

"Go back to sleep, Three. I've got it from here."

Her words go unheard, as Three had passed out as soon as he laid down. She smiles some more before walking out of the shed, stretching more as she leaves.

She makes sure that the campfire continues strong before she sits down, enjoying it's warmth. She looks towards the sky, watching the stars. She absently plays with her necklace, thinking back to what Serena said earlier about her race.

"A High Elf, huh? Do we resemble them so?" She muses, chuckling.

She stands after staring at the sky for a half an hour, then checks on the horses. Her horse was standing, watching her approach while the other two laid down.

She pets his nose when she reaches him. "You got stuck with the watch too, huh bud?"

Cider nickers. Valindra chuckles.

"I understand." She continues to pet him, before she feels cramps in her shoulder blades. She shrugs, asking Cider rhetorically: "You won't tell anyone if I remove my cloak, will you?"

Pale light filters into the shed through cracks in the walls. Serena and Three both wake up to find that Valindra had covered them in blankets. They walk out of the shed, Three rubbing his eyes, to see Valindra stirring the stew pot.

"What time is it?" Three yawns.

"I'd say it's about six in the morning." Valindra says, looking towards the east. She loads up their bowls. "I hope you're hungry. Today, we tackle the manor."

Chapter 4

Into the Manor

Part 1

*S*erena closes her pack and throws it over her shoulder, then grabs

her shield before also throwing it over her shoulder. Three searches

through his pack, making sure that he has everything that he needs.

Valindra dumps a bucket of water into the trough, that she had found

throughout her shift, so that the horses have water while they're inside.

She places the bucket back beside the well before joining her party at the

gate.

"Everyone ready?" Serena asks.

"Aye!" Three caws.

Valindra nods. "Aye."

They leave the garden, latching the gate behind them. They turn to

the manor. It looms over them. They start walking towards it.

"It's not so scary in the daylight." Three thinks out loud.

"Even graveyards are not so scary in the daylight. Doesn't mean that they are not dangerous." Valindra remarks.

When they reach the front door, Serena stops her party. "Why is the door ajar?"

"The door is a door, not a jar."

Three caws in laughter at Valindra's joke. She looks rather proud of herself.

Serena glares at Valindra, not appreciative of her joke. "I was asking why the door is slightly open."

"Then why not ask that?" Serena rolls her eyes at Valindra. Valindra breathes deeply, becoming serious again. "The Cliffbane boy probably didn't close the door all the way when he went in. I think we should - "

Before she has a chance of finishing her sentence, Three opens the door further, then walks in. A second or two passes, before he reappears in the doorway.

"I don't have to invite you two in, do I?"

Three disappears into the house again. Valindra passes by Serena as she walks in. Serena's shoulders slump forward in defeat.

"So, no plan, then." She straightens her posture before walking into the manor.

The main entrance is in complete disarray. Part of the upstairs balcony railing lies on the downstairs floor, books and other debris littering

the rest of the floor. What can be seen of the carpet shows that it is torn.
Dust covers everything. Light filtering in through a hole in the roof
illuminates part of the floor. Three stands next to where the light shines.

He points to the illuminated floor, looking towards the girls. "Don't
step there. Weather damage."

Serena scoffs in disgust. "This place is a pigsty!"

Valindra trudges through the debris, her nose scrunching in
repulsion. "A pigsty is cleaner than this."

Three moves further into the house. His head swivels as he looks at
his surroundings.

"There's three different hallways. Should we split up?"

"We should really stay together." Serena says, carefully picking her
way through the debris.

Three turns to look at her. "Why?"

"She's right, Three." They both turn to look at Valindra. "We don't
know what dangers are lurking around the corners."

Three cocks his head. "You know, Val, you're like the 'mom' of the
party. And Serena's the 'over-protective sister'."

"Excuse you? Where is this coming from?" Serena sounds rather
unhappy at his statement. So what if she was trying to keep them safe? If
either one of them got hurt while up there with her, her father would be
pissed that she went there with people not on the Watch.

Valindra stops, thinking for a moment. "No, no, he has a point."

Serena looks at her as if she had three heads. She couldn't believe that Valindra was siding with Three on this.

Three beams. "So, which way, Val-mom?"

Valindra and Serena continue making their way over to Three, stepping over the debris and pieces of the railing. They finally reach him, taking a moment to shake the smaller debris from their boots. Valindra looks around her, inspecting the hallways as much as she can from where she stands. She looks first to the left, then to her right, before finally looking straight ahead.

"Let's go to the right. It looks like it might be the shortest hallway."

She takes the lead, the other two following behind her, down the right hallway. They come across two closed doors, one on either side of the hall. Valindra tries the right door, and it creaks open. She prepares to draw her rapier before walking in. Three and Serena also get ready to draw their swords, following Valindra into the room.

The room is in almost as bad shape, if not worse, than the main entrance. Books and papers line the floor. A desk is turned over against the wall on the other side of the room. The window beside the desk is smashed. The party stands there, shock across their faces.

"What the hell happened here?" Serena asks.

"I'm guessing that someone was looking for something." Valindra answers. She walks over to the furthest wall, glass crunching under her feet the closer to the window she gets. She looks out of the window. "The window was broken from the outside."

"Maybe it was from that ghostly laughing that Misses Cliffbane was talking about?" Three voices.

"How would that have worked?" Serena asks Three.

Three shrugs his shoulders, not knowing the answer.

Valindra answers for him as she kneels to inspect the desk. "It could have boomed. Or it could be from the rock over by the bookcase."

The other two look around, finally finding the rock. Valindra continues to investigate the desk. It is mostly broken, but one drawer remains intact. She tries to open it, but it doesn't budge.

"Locked. Hey, Three, can you carefully make your way over here and open this?"

"Aye-aye, Val-mom!"

Three hops his way over to Valindra, being careful around the broken glass, and removes his pack once he gets to her. He opens his pack and rummages for a few seconds, before removing his thieves' tools. He sets his pack aside and starts working on the locked drawer once he found his tools.

"I tried to make sure that my tools were at the top of my pack this morning, but they must have moved around while I was hopping." Three explained.

Valindra pats the top of his head proudly. "That was a very good idea, Three!"

Three smiles wide as he continues working on the lock. Serena moves papers around with her foot, making her way into the room.

"Don't praise him as he's picking a lock!"

Valindra narrows her eyes at Serena. "He's doing more than you are."

Serena's eyes also narrow. She huffs before bending to pick up a handful of papers. She examines them, reading them quickly and turning them over.

"These look to be from random books. Whoever did this was looking for something specific."

The lock on the drawer clicks. Three pulls his tools out of the lock and puts them away in their case, before putting them back in his pack. Valindra pulls on the drawer and looks at the contents.

"There's only papers in here…" She takes the papers out and closes the drawer. She quickly scans the papers. "This is the deed to the house."

Serena walks over and crouches behind Valindra, also scanning the papers. "Whoever made this mess was probably looking for this. We should return them to Misses Cliffbane."

"Agreed. Three, can you – "

Three shushes them. They look at him, and find him close to the doorway, peeking into the hall. Valindra reopens the drawer and puts the papers back, carefully closing it, trying not to make any noise. They can hear a man mumbling but can't quite make out what he's saying. Serena stands and tries to move quietly, but a floorboard creaks under her weight. She winces quietly.

"What was that?" His words were clear that time.

They can hear him stomping closer. Valindra puts her hand on the hilt of her dagger. Just as he appears in the doorway, she throws her dagger. It lands in his right thigh. He grunts, but it's enough to draw his attention to them.

Serena darts her eyes to Three, finding him quietly drawing his rapier. "Get him, Three!"

The big guy looks beside him, just as Three leaves a gaping slash against his chest. He grunts again, this time seeking support from the doorframe. He brings a hand up to his chest. Serena takes this opportunity to close the distance between them, burying her longsword into his shoulder. With one last grunt, he drops to the ground, dead.

She smiles. "Hey, that was – "

Three pushes her from behind, and lands partially in the hallway, partially on top of the dead body.

"Why did you do that?!" Three almost yells at her, half angry.

"I should be the one asking you that! Why did you push me?"

"I could have killed him had he not seen me! And you ruined that when you called out to me!" Three was angry.

"I was trying to encourage you!"

Three lunges towards Serena, but Valindra catches him. She separates the two of them.

"Enough! Both of you! You've probably alerted everyone else on or below this floor of our presence!"

If there was one thing that Serena didn't like about this situation, it was seeing Valindra angry. She could now see why Three that of her as the mom of their party.

"Three, I want you to apologize for pushing Serena. And you," Valindra turns to look at Serena. "Get your head out of your ass. You're smarter than this."

Three crosses his arms and looks away from Serena. He pouts as best as he can. "I'm sorry."

Serena stands, wiping the dust from her pants. "I'm sorry, too. I should have let you attack the enemy instead of alerting him to your presence."

"That's better." Valindra takes her dagger out of the body, wiping the blood off on the body before sheathing it. "Three, are you able to carry the deed in your pack?"

Three perks up. "Sure thing, Val-mom!" He hops back over to the desk.

"I see now that he was right in his earlier statement. About you being the mother of our party."

"Someone has to make sure that we don't slit the other's throats." Valindra looks at Serena. "He was right about you, too. Or at least half right. You two act like siblings, from what I've observed."

Serena nods in agreement. She didn't know if most siblings acted the way they do. Her and her brother never acted that way. She also didn't know if Valindra had any experience with siblings or not. They didn't know much about each other, so she thought that this might have been too early in their partnership to talk about anything in their personal lives.

Three rejoins them. "Got all the papers, Val-mom."

"Good. Onto the next room."

They walk across the hall and are about to turn the handle, when they hear a voice.

"Hello?"

Valindra motions for them to be silent, but Three doesn't take the hint. He presses the side of his head to the door.

"Hello? Are you behind the door?"

"What door? I'm in the room at the end of the hall!"

Valindra draws her rapier, holding it steady as she motions to the other two to follow behind her. Three and Serena move behind her, and they slowly make their way towards the end of the hall.

"Are you coming or not?" The voice asks, quite grumpily. "If so, could you please hurry up? This rope is chaffing against my wrists."

Valindra stops, causing Three to bump into her. She stumbles forward a little, sighs, before an eyebrow raises towards the end of the hall. "Wait, you're tied up?"

"Yes!"

"Are you friend or foe?"

"Friend! Now, please hurry up!"

The party look to each other, a silent question passing among them. Valindra nods, and they make their way to the room.

When they enter, they find a red-skinned Tiefling tied up, sitting cross-legged, and in nothing but his undergarments. His right eye is partially closed, the result of a black eye. His lip is busted. There is a large bruise covering the left side of his ribcage, the blooming purple and black a stark contrast to his skin tone.

"Please excuse my, um, lack of appropriate attire. They stripped me and threw my clothing into a room back in that hallway when I was brought here."

Valindra sheaths her rapier as she walks over to him. She unsheathes her dagger when she reaches him, walking around him. Kneeling behind him, she sets to work on cutting the rope around his wrists.

"Much appreciated."

"You're welcome. What is your name?"

Serena answers for him. "Leucious Creed. Necromancy wizard. Thirty-three years old, I do believe." One of the bindings snaps, as Valindra looks at Serena, standing at the entrance, in a questioning manner. "My father arrested him five years ago for smuggling."

Three looks to his right before wandering off in that direction.

"Ah, so you're the Stoutbrow girl." Serena only glares at him. "Your father was right to bring me in. But no need to worry about me now. I have done my sentence."

"Then why are you here?" She asks him.

The second binding snaps. Valindra moves to kneel in front of Leucious, setting to work on freeing his legs. He brings his wrists in front of him, rubbing them. Rope burns show purple against his skin.

"I was just starting to turn my life around for the better when I was ambushed on the way to check ticket prices for a ship. Chrom wanted me to rejoin him in his business. I refused. And I ended up in this state."

"No, why are you here, in this room, practically naked?"

The rope snaps, and Valindra sheathes her dagger. She helps Leucious to stand.

"As I stated already, they stripped me of my clothing when I first arrived here. As to why I'm in this room, Chrom brought me up here to try to convince me to join him. For the third time. I was about to refuse, but then one of you made a ruckus down the hall and caught his attention."

Serena narrows her eyes even more. She had a gut feeling that him being here wasn't a good thing.

"Are you good to stand on your own?" Valindra asks, his arm over her shoulders.

"Yes, thank you."

He removes his arm. Valindra walks away and begins investigating the room. Three also walks around, checking corners and bookshelves. Valindra spots two doors, one on either side of the room, and crosses the room to try them. They were locked.

"How did you get in this room? Both of the doors here lead outside of the manor, and you didn't pass by us in the hallway."

Three stands about six feet away from Valindra. He's still investigating the room. Leucious is about to answer, when a scream reverberates around the room. Serena and Leucious cover their ears and look towards the source of the scream. They see Three jump away from an immaculately clean area rug, his feathers ruffled in fright. Valindra catches Three as he jumps and pulls him away from the rug. The scream stops. Valindra holds Three close to her, his little feathers shaking. The other two lower their hands.

Three caws in fright. "What the fuck was that?!"

"That was an illusion spell." Leucious answers.

Serena draws her longsword and moves toward Leucious. She backs him into the closest wall, sword point at his throat.

"You know that because you cast it as a trap, did you not?" She accuses him.

"What? No!" He holds his hands up in defense. "I know this because I witnessed Chrom force another magic user to place it on the trapdoor under the rug! He had it set so that it would activate if anyone other than him approached the door. He also killed the poor bugger."

Valindra continues to coddle Three. "Serena, back down!"

"He's a criminal! How can we trust him?"

"If he weren't on our side, he would have taken my dagger as I was freeing him. And do you see that bruise on his ribs? It looks to have been a serious injury. And he's nearly nude. You would have to be an idiot to try to attack while injured and nude."

"I was punched. It hurt like a bitch, even during the healing process." Leucious explains.

Valindra looks sorry for the naked Tiefling, before her face returns to normal. "Come now, Serena. Lower your sword. That is an order."

"Damn orders." Serena mutters under her breath. She begrudgingly lowers her sword.

"Good. Leucious, come along with us. Let's find your clothes."

They make their way back out into the hallway. Serena takes the lead, as Valindra has Three partially under her cloak. They also stay in the middle, to keep Serena separated from Leucious. They reach the two doorways, Leucious seeing the body.

"Looks like you had no issue with Chrom."

"That's the guy who beat you up?" Three pipes up, no longer shaking.

Three removes himself from Valindra and goes over to Chrom. He starts rummaging through his pockets.

Chapter 5

Into the Manor

Part 2

"Hmm. Nothing in his pockets. He only had his coin purse on him."

The group opens the purse and divide everything between them.

"That's two copper, ten gold, and a platinum apiece. I will hold onto your share until we find your clothes, Leucious." Valindra pockets their coins.

"Thank you, my lady." He turns and points at the other door. "My clothing should be in that room."

They all stand outside the door, Valindra handing Leucious her dagger. Serena reaches for the doorknob, wrapping her hand around it. She looks at her party, who are waiting, ready for anything. She looks at Valindra. Valindra nods, giving her the go-ahead. Serena nods back before returning her attention to the door. The knob turned; she opens the door to…

… a nearly empty room?

The adventurer's walk in, confused. They look around; there's a pile of clothes in the back right corner and a chest along the back wall, but nothing else. Why would a single chest and clothing be the only things in the room?

"I'd know that cloth anywhere." Leucious claims, recognizing some of the fabric.

Leucious goes over to the pile of clothing, rooting through it before pulling out his black leather pants. Valindra investigates the wall to her left, checking for hidden cracks with her fingers. Serena copies her, investigating the right wall.

Leucious has pulled on his pants, his billowy lavender shirt and his sleeveless tunic that ends around mid-thigh. He attempts to balance on his booted right foot, trying to put on his left boot. Loosing his balance, he lands in the pile of clothes, before popping back up wearing an azure leather trench coat, his boot now on. He continues to adjust his coat's cuffs.

While the others are doing their respective things, Three stares at the chest. He approaches it, almost like he's being drawn to it. He reaches out, not hearing the low rumble.

Valindra picks up on the noise, turning her head in the direction that it was coming from. She sees Three, reaching for the chest, seeming to ignore the rumbling noise. Something doesn't seem right….

She notices the light glinting off a liquid seeping from the chest. She tries to warn him: "Three, watch ou-"

Her warning comes too late. The chest opens, a blue-purple tongue popping out of it. Its sharp teeth bite down, but Three is quicker, jumping back, its teeth closing on nothing. Three draws his rapier, a quick slash coming down against the chest. Valindra moves forward, readying her rapier, when Leucious acts first.

"Magic Missile!"

Three magical bolts fly in spirals from his right hand, hitting the mimic. It screeches, the sound of rusty hinges.

Serena moves forward, but slowly, almost like she was in a daze. The mimic lashes out with it tongue, grappling Three, his sword clattering as it hits the ground. He struggles in the mimic's grasp, his efforts failing him. Valindra, her own rapier drawn, slashes at the mimic, but it seems unfazed.

Leucious spots a corner of his spell book under more cloth. He picks it up and flips through its pages, looking for an appropriate spell. He's hesitant on casting the one he was looking for, but casts it anyway.

"Ray of Frost." He casts, his voice cool.

The room grows colder, a blue-white beam shooting from his outstretched hand. It flies overtop the mimic, narrowly missing Serena's head as she moved closer.

"Watch where you're casting!" She nearly shouts, pissed off, drawing her longsword.

A sorry look crosses Leucious's face. Serena slashes at the mimic. It screeches louder than before, a purple liquid oozing from the wound. With this new wound, Three manages to escape its grasp, covered in slime, as he picks up his sword. Valindra attacks again, more of that purple substance oozing out.

Leucious raises his hand again, more confident this time. "Let's try this again, shall we? Ray of Frost!"

Another blue-white beam streams from his hand, hitting the mimic square in its side. With a yell from Serena, she arches her longsword over her head, landing the killing blow. The mimics tongue drops to the ground, cut off from the body.

Valindra walks over to Three, then kneels.

"Are you okay?" She reaches out, then jerks her hand back before she touches him. "Oh, gods, you're covered in slime."

"I'm okay. Freaking mimics." He grumbles. "I'm going to go outside and shake this slime off." He walks to the door, then looks over his shoulder. "I want to keep the tongue. Then folks will believe me when I say that I survived a mimic." Looking forward, he walks out of the room.

Serena's eyebrows furrow. "The tongue of a mimic is a weird thing to want to keep."

"Maybe he'll use it as a spell ingredient." Leucious offers as an answer.

"A trophy." They look to Valindra. "He wants to commemorate his first battle, where he came very close to danger." She stands.

Serena quirks an eyebrow. "A trophy? Why do you sound so sure of that?"

"I understand all too well about almost becoming good acquaintances with Death."

She pulls at a leather cord around her neck, revealing a tooth at the end of her necklace. The other two look at it, trying to guess as to what it could have come from.

"This is from my first battle, about four-hundred years ago. The left incisor of an adult white dragon."

"It makes for beautiful jewelry." Serena states, impressed.

"A white dragon's tooth? From four-hundred years ago?" Leucious is sceptical. "For starters, that is well preserved. For another, how old are you?"

"A rather rude question to ask a lady. But I shall indulge you. I am four-hundred-and-fifty years old. As I stated, it has been about four-hundred years. It has actually been three-hundred-and-fifty years since I slayed my first dragon."

Leucious is in awe. "Awesome."

"Can we investigate the mimic?" Serena asks, growing impatient.

The three of them surround the lifeless mimic. Valindra opens the lid, only to find a skeletal arm covered in ripped cloth.

"Sweet! Bones that I can grind down!" Leucious snatches it, the cloth falling from it.

Serena picks up the cloth. "We could probably use this to wrap around the tongue."

Having found his satchel in the pile of cloth, Leucious works on grinding down the bones. Serena wraps the mimic's tongue in the cloth. Valindra stands by the door, keeping watch.

"I hope that nothing has happened to Three."

Serena stands, moving to beside Valindra. "He is alright, Valindra. He's a human-sized bird of prey. Besides, he would have squawked by now if there were any issues."

"Who would've done what in what now?" Three asks, appearing at the door.

"Valindra was just worried about you, that's all."

"Awe, Val-mom!" He hugs Valindra. "I knew you cared!"

Valindra is momentarily stunned. She shakes her head, placing an arm around Three's back. She smooths down the feathers on the top of his head with her other hand, almost as if she were petting him.

"Of course I care, Three. I wouldn't be a very good mother if I didn't." She was smiling. The thought of being a mother had never occurred to her before. She could probably get used to it.

Three makes a chortling noise and snuggles his head more against Valindra. His eyes pop open for a moment, though, before closing again. Valindra stiffens a little, a look not quite of concern crossing her face before she relaxes once more. Although quick, Serena notices how uncomfortable she seemed. Almost as if Valindra were hiding something.

What is she hiding? Did Three just discover whatever it is that she's hiding?

She shakes these thoughts from her head as Leucious stands beside her.

"So, team, what's the plan?" He asks.

Her mood turns sour once more. "It doesn't involve you, criminal." Serena nearly spits.

"I just helped you take down an enemy!"

"Does not mean anything!"

"Serena, drop it." Valindra stops the argument before it has a chance to really start. She still holds Three, or maybe he's still holding her? She addresses Leucious. "Welcome to the party. We're searching the manor and making sure that it is clear and safe enough for the owners to return home."

"Sounds good to me. Shall we go and explore?" He asks.

"Yes, we should." She lets go of Three. He holds onto her a little longer before letting go.

Serena holds out the cloth-wrapped tongue to Three, seeming upset with Valindra. "The mimic's tongue."

"Thanks!" He takes the tongue from her and opens his pack, placing the tongue in it. He closes his pack, throws it onto his back, and walks out the door.

The rest of the party follows, congregating in the hallway. Leucious and Three take the lead, walking back to the foyer, about ten feet in front of Valindra and Serena.

"Why do you trust him so much?" Serena whispers to Valindra.

"I don't trust him as much as you think I do. I'm trying to earn his trust and loyalty by displaying my trust to him." She explains, keeping her tone hushed.

"But we hardly know him or what his intentions might be."

"That's why I didn't tell him everything."

Serena chuckles. "Bold choice. Smart move."

They both laugh quietly. Hearing their laughter, Leucious turns and looks at them, his eyebrow raised in a questioning manner.

"Are you two good?"

"We're fine, Leucious." Valindra informs him. She changes the subject. "How long is this hallway? We've been walking for a while, and we haven't come across any doors."

"We passed the foyer and went straight down the next hallway. We will be coming to the only door down this hall in a few moments. The library is the only room down this way."

Valindra makes a mental note. *How does he know what room is down here?*

The rest of the journey down the hall is silent. They reach the end of the hall, the only opening on their left. However, the door, or what's left of the door, hangs on the hinges.

Serena reaches for her sword hilt. "Why is the door broken?"

Leucious was wondering the same thing. "That's a good question, Stoutbrow."

All Serena could feel for him was hatred. He treads on all her nerves.

The party quietly makes their way into the library, Serena and Valindra taking the lead. The library is dark, presumably from closed curtains. Serena and Three can't see much, but Valindra and Leucious find that there are books laying on the floor, tattered.

Valindra quietly draws her rapier. She whispers: "Be on your guard, everyone."

Serena readies her sword and pulls her shield off her back. They walk in further. Serena steps on a broken tabletop, the weakened wood cracking more. A low growl resonates close by. They stop moving.

"What was that?" Three asks. He had no sense of when to whisper.

A large hound, black and red in colour, rounds the corner of a nearby bookshelf. It growls again. Serena, basing where to swing from its growls, attacks, swinging her longsword above her head. She strikes. A deeper growl resonates from the hell hound.

Valindra attacks next, her sword whizzing past the hound's shoulder as it steps aside. It lunges at her, and she barely pulls her arm back in time to miss its gnashing teeth. It barks and growls at her.

Three moves closer to the front of the party, amped for another fight. "Where is it?"

He does not wait for an answer; he swings blindly. He only knows that he hit the hell hound when it yelps. Blood starts to trickle down from its other shoulder, where Three was able to pierce it.

"Lucky shot, mate!" Leucious congratulates, setting aside his book. He walks over to a nearby bookshelf. It stands at ten feet tall and five feet wide. He pulls a handful of slightly glowing moss from his component pouch and touches the bookcase. "But why don't we shed some light on the adversary?"

Dim light spreads outward in a twenty-foot radius. It is enough to illuminate the hell hound.

"Ah, that's better." Serena states. She swings at the hound, but it moves aside.

While it moves, Valindra moves, piercing its left flank. It roars. The hound stumbles closer to Leucious. Three stares at the beast. His bottom beak drops open, his jaw agape in surprise.

"Is that what we've been fighting the whole time?"

Another blue-white beam flies from Leucious's hands. It hits the hound square in its left shoulder. It stumbles away from Leucious.

"Ray of Frost. And yes. A beautiful creature, is it not?" There is a hint of sarcasm in Leucious's statement.

Not waiting for another attack from the creature, Serena attacks, slashing at the hell hound. It drops to the ground, dead, bleeding from the wound across its back.

"What the hell was that?" Three asks.

"That was a hell hound." Leucious answers him.

Valindra sheaths her rapier, asking aloud: "Why the hell was there a hell hound here?"

"Honestly?" The party looks at Leucious, who is still standing by the bookshelf, his hands on his hips. "I think that he belonged to the magic user that Chrom killed."

"So why was it still here if he's dead?" Serena asks.

Valindra puts a hand to her chin, rubbing it in thought. "If the mutt did indeed belong to that deceased magic user, then they were probably separated when Chrom had him brought here. The beast would have been searching for its…" She pauses, thinking, before looking to Leucious for clarification. "Its master? Friend? How does that work again?"

"It would have been his animal companion, so friend would be the right option."

Valindra's jaw locks, her mouth set in a straight line as she nods.

"Well, then, is everyone all right? Does anyone need to rest?"

"I'm good. In fact, I feel, oh, what's the word? Less… squishy?" Leucious states.

Three shakes his head, his feathers ruffling before smoothing down. "I'm fine. Just surprised is all."

"You must feel braver after facing the hound, Leucious. It's only bravado." Serena states, sheathing her sword and shield. She rests her hand on the hilt of her sword. "What about you, Valindra? You came close to losing your hand to the hell hound."

Valindra rolls her shoulders. "Better than ever. I feel much more invigorated."

"That's settled, then. Where everyone is healthy and not requiring a rest, I think that we should continue to search the manor."

"Excellent idea, Stoutbrow! Come then, young Three! Let us walk ahead of the ladies and keep them safe!" Leucious exclaims, the bravado that Serena mentioned earlier showing through.

"Aye-aye, old man!" Three caws excitedly. Leucious's ego deflates at his remark about his age.

Three walks out ahead of everyone, Leucious following behind in a slump. Serena and Valindra laugh at his reaction. They calm down, Valindra looking at Serena and placing a firm hand on her shoulder.

"Everyone agrees. Good thinking. You will make a great captain one day."

Serena blushes at her compliment. "I don't think so. I am not comfortable with giving orders."

"You will never move up in rank if you cannot give orders." Valindra advises. "But rest assured, you will, eventually, grow comfortable enough to command an army."

Serena chuckles. "What are you, a witch? Are you able to see the future?"

Valindra only smiles. She leads Serena out of the library and down the hall. They meet up with Leucious and Three in the main foyer.

"Where to, Val-mom?"

"I don't know, Three. Serena, where do you think we should go?"

....

Back in town, Misses Cliffbane walks out of her house, a laundry basket with wet bedding on her hip. She walks around the side of the house and sets the basket down. She throws a few sheets over the line before she stops and turns in the direction of the manor. She brings her hand up to her chest, clenched in a loose fist.

"Please find him, adventurers. Bring my Thadeus home safely." She prays to no one in particular.

Chapter 6

The Upper Story

*S*erena's eyes widen as she looks at Valindra.

"Me? Oh, it doesn't matter what I think. You choose." She tells her. Why would Valindra leave it to her to choose where to go?

"No, no, my opinion matters not. Where should we go, Serena? Should we go left?" She grabs Serena's chin and tilts her head to the left, looking down the long, dark hallway. "Or should we go up?" She then turns her head towards the staircase, then whispers in her ear. "The choice is yours. So make your damn decision and command us."

Is she trying to help me decide where to go? Serena thinks. Valindra hadn't removed her hand from her chin yet. *Why would she tell me to choose when she's practically telling me where our party should go? Unless…*

"Um…" She hesitates. She hated being put on the spot. "I think that we should go… up?"

"Is that a question? Or are you commanding us?" Valindra asks, still whispering.

Nope. She's just being a bitch.

Serena breathes in deeply through her nose. She squares her shoulders before looking at her party. "Upstairs. We go upstairs." No hesitation that time.

Three shrugs his shoulders. "Whatever you say."

He and Leucious walk towards the staircase. Valindra finally removes her hand from Serena's chin and pats her on the shoulder. Serena looks at Valindra.

"See? That wasn't so hard." Valindra walks away, headed for the stairs. Three and Leucious have already started walking up.

Serena lets out a shaky breath, her shoulders rounding as she slouches. Her eyes close. *Maybe she was trying to help me.* Her inner tone changes. *She could have been nicer about it, though.*

"Serena?" She opens her eyes and looks at Valindra. With one hand on the banister and one foot starting up, she found Valindra looking at her. "Come along; we're wasting daylight."

Serena nods once. "Right." She stands straighter before joining Valindra at the base of the stairs.

Leucious is halfway up the stairs, with Three close to the top of the stairs, as the girls start making their way up. A board creaks. Leucious falls forward suddenly, his weight breaking one of the stairs.

Three turns around and looks down at him. "Goodness, are you alright?"

"I'm fine. Just caught by surprise, is all." Leucious answers. He pushes himself up, avoiding the broken stairs once he gets up. He turns to look at the girls behind him. "Watch out for that step, girls. It's rotted more than the others."

They give him a thumbs up. They finish their journey up the staircase, Three hopping around on the landing, waiting for them.

Valindra notices how Leucious is keeping his weight off his right leg. She gestures to his leg, silently asking how he is. He assures her that he's alright, signalling 'ok' with his hand. Once he's good to walk again, they move to the first corner, the one on their right, guided by the bit of light from the hole in the ceiling. Three and Valindra look around the corner.

"Nothing around the corner." Valindra informs her party, turning back to them. As she's turning, she notices an unlit torch on the banister behind Leucious. Pointing at it, she instructs him: "Leucious, grab that torch. Three, get out your flint and steel."

Three takes his pack off and begins to rummage through it, looking for his flint and steel. Leucious has a little trouble with removing the torch, the metal screeching once it's been freed. He removes the spiderwebs from the inside of it.

"What are you planning to do with a torch?" Serena asks Valindra.

Leucious held the torch as Three attempted to light it. "We're going to use it to light the other torches so that you and Three can see."

The torch ignites. Valindra looks around, spotting another torch from the wall six feet away from her. She takes it over to the other torch and ignites it, the spiderwebs burning away in little sparks.

"We should split into two groups. We'll light the torches down this hallway first."

"I'm going with Val-mom!" Three exclaims cheerfully.

He starts down the hall, the torch held high in front of him. Valindra moves to follow, but Serena grabs her by her bicep.

"Do not make me partner up with Leucious." She whispers to her.

"Are you expecting me to say no to a three-year-old?" She whispers back. "We'll be right across the hall from you two."

Begrudgingly, Serena removes her hand. Valindra hands her the torch. She takes it and stands beside Leucious.

Who just happens to speak up. "I'm sorry, Val, but is it such a clever idea to split up?"

"Perhaps not, but you and I are the only ones who can see in the dark. The other half of us need to be able to see, as well."

She turns the corner, following Three. She stops a few feet away from her starting point, turning back to look at Leucious. "And just so we're clear, Three is the only one allowed to call me 'Val'."

She walks away. Leucious is taken aback by her statement, and when he turns to ask Serena about it, he finds that she is also surprised. They look at each other, shrugging when they can't figure it out.

Leucious offers to take the torch for her, but Serena pushes past. He follows her, attempting to at least stick to the plan.

As they approach the first torch, Leucious asks Serena: "So what happened back there? When Val asked you about where we should go?"

"Oh, that? I guess she was getting me to command the party." She reaches the lit torch to the other one, but Leucious takes it from her. He ignites it for her, reaching a little higher than she can.

The torch on the wall ignites. Leucious lowers the torch as he asks Serena his next question. "I thought Val was leading the party. Why would she get you to command us?"

Serena grabs the torch back from him before pushing past him, continuing down the hall to find the next torch. Leucious rolls his eyes, breaking into a light jog to catch up to her.

"I don't know why she would get me to command the party. And if she's leading us, then she assumed that position herself." Serena stretches onto her tiptoes to reach the next torch when they approached it, but she couldn't quite reach the top of it. "Maybe," her voice straining from the stretching, "a few centuries on the battlefield has taught her a few things about leadership."

Leucious wraps his hand around the torch, silently asking to take it and light the other one for her. She drops her hand, and he lights it, only to find her glaring at him once he lowers his arm.

"What? Why are you looking at me like that?"

"I could have gotten that myself." She crosses her arms over her chest.

"You were struggling on the tips of your toes trying to reach it. I thought that I would be the good guy, like the gentleman that I am, and help you out."

"Would you two stop bickering?" Valindra asks them from the end of the hallway. They look towards the sound of her voice, only to find that her and Three had made their way down to the end of the hall. "You're bound to wake the dead from how loud you're being."

Serena glowers some more but makes her way over to the two of them, who are illuminated by both the light of the torch and the light filtering in through the dirty window. Leucious follows her, shaking his head.

The party regroups by the window. Standing outside of a door, Valindra and Leucious find some holders on the wall above and place their torches in them.

Three places his hand on the door handle. He looks at the party. Serena readies her sword and shield, Leucious opens his spell book, and Valindra has her hand on the hilt of her sword. Valindra counts to three with the fingers of her right hand. Three opens the door when she raises her third finger. Serena charges in as soon as the door opens and stands in the middle of the bathroom.

She lowers her sword and shield and walks out of the room. "Bathroom's all clean." She was embarrassed; she should have known better than to just run head-first into an unknown area. "Where to now?"

"There's another set of doors right there." Three says, pointing at the doors on his right. "Should we investigate what's behind them?"

"We probably should." Valindra says, walking to the doors. "It means that there would be less places for an enemy to hide."

She reaches the doors, Three joining her. Leucious motions for Serena to go ahead of him. She rolls her eyes at him, but walks ahead anyway, with Leucious taking up the back of the party. Behind them, blue-spotted yellow tentacles descend from the ceiling. They creep their way around Leucious, pinning his arms to his sides. He cries out, but it's cut short, the tentacles paralyzing him.

The rest of the party turns at the noise. Valindra, her hand still on the hilt of her rapier, draws it, ever ready. She looks around but sees nothing around them. Finally, she looks at the tentacles and follow them up.

"What the hell is that?" She asks, spotting the creature.

Serena follows her gaze, also spotting the creature. Her eyes widen, both fascinated and a little scared. Her sword and shield clatter to the floor as she drops them and grabs her crossbow. She knocks a bolt in it and shoots at the beast, it screaming as the bolt sticks into it.

Three, thankful that they had lit the torches, also spotted the creature, and drew his short bow and an arrow from his quiver. He shoots, and the arrow flies, hitting the creature in its right eye. It screams again.

Valindra rushes forward, more concerned with the tentacles encircling Leucious, and slashes down. The tentacles go limp and hang around Leucious as she severed them from the body of the beast. It screams once more. Leucious falls, a heavy thud on the floor, as he no longer has the support of the tentacles to hold him up.

The crawling creature drops to the ground, five feet from Valindra and Leucious. It looks at Valindra with four pink eyes, a seething primal hate showing through them. She could see and feel, at the back of her mind, that this creature was the top predator in whatever ecosystem it thrived in. Valindra holds her rapier, poised to parry its attack. She falters, though, as the creature lurches at her and bites her left shoulder. She cries out in pain.

Almost as if her cry were waking him up, Leucious jumps up, stumbling, but able to stand his ground. The tentacles hang loosely around his arms, and he looks at them, confusion written on his face.

"Where the hell did these come from?" He asks.

A bolt flies past him, narrowly missing his nose. He follows the bolt and spots the beast, the bolt hitting it. He also spots Valindra, holding her shoulder. The creature only growls.

"A pandimensional beast attacked you. You were paralyzed by it." Serena tells him, knocking another bolt.

Three knocks another arrow but hesitates before he shoots; he didn't want to accidentally hit Val. He was scared that she would be mad at him if he hit her. The arrow goes wide and misses it target, landing in the floor about three feet from it.

Valindra swings, hissing through her teeth at the sharp, searing pain shooting down her arm. Her sword whispers by where the beast's tentacles once were. Her sword drops from her hand, point down, in front of her. Valindra grips her shoulder more. The crawler lurches at her again.

But it misses Valindra as Leucious calls out the name of his spell again, and it's hit in the face by a blue-white beam. Valindra looks at Leucious. She's thankful, but he can only see the hint of thankfulness through the amount of pain showing on her face.

"I thank you. I probably could not have taken another hit from it."

A bolt whizzes between the two of them as Serena takes her shot. It lands between the pandimensional beast's eyes, and it gives out one last scream before going limp, dead. Serena makes her way towards its corpse.

"It was the least that I could do. You did save my life, after all." Leucious says. He starts to make his way over to her, but Three nearly tramples over him as he hops over to Valindra.

"Val-mom! Are you okay?" He's panicked.

She removes her hand from her shoulder. She rolls her shoulder, wincing at the pain. "I've survived worse. The bleeding will stop soon. We should continue searching the manor." She grabs her sword with her right hand, switching from her normal hand. "Is everyone good to move on?"

Serena returns to the group and hands Three his arrows. They put away their ammunition. Making sure to pick up her sword and shield, she waits by the doors for the rest of her party. Leucious joins her. Three walks alongside Valindra, worry etching his face.

"Let's just get this over with." Valindra says once they join the other two. "Open the damn door."

Leucious opens the door. Serena raises her sword and shield and walks into the room. The others pile in behind her.

Toys are scattered about the room, some of them broken. Papers line the floor as books are scattered from the bookshelf. Trunks lay open around the room. The bed in the corner is made, a muddy stuffed rabbit sitting on top of the covers.

An audible sigh comes from Leucious when he spots the rabbit. Valindra and Serena both look at him before they return to scanning their surroundings.

"All clear." Serena lowers her sword and shield.

Three walks away from the group, making his way to the bed. He peers into the trunk at the foot of the bed, shrugging as he decides to ignore it. He makes his way to the head of the bed and picks up the stuffed rabbit.

"What are you doing?" Serena asks him.

"Taking this stuffed toy."

"We're not thieves, Three." Valindra lightly scolds him.

"I'll be giving it back!" He walks back over to them, showing them the rabbit. "Look! There's mud on it!"

Leucious makes his way over to the bookcase. "So? That just means that someone got it dirty when they were playing with it."

Realization dawns on Valindra's face. "It belongs to the Cliffbane child."

Misses Cliffbane's voice repeats in her head, faded. "*My son had dropped his stuffed rabbit...*"

Valindra looks around the room. "This must have been his room. Whoever was in here cared about the bed being made and the rabbit visible, but not the rest."

Serena walks around the smaller corner of the wall taking up space in the room. "There's another door here."

"Probably the closet."

Serena opens the door just a crack and peers in past it. She closes the door again before rejoining the party.

"You were right. Nothing interesting in there. Clothes strewn about."

Valindra thinks. *What was Chrom looking for?* She addresses Three. "Three, pack the toy. We'll return it to the boy once we find him."

"Aye-aye, Val-mom!"

At the same time, Leucious questions her, the book in his hands forgotten. "When we find what boy? You told me that we were ensuring the safety of the manor before the owners return."

"I..." she hesitates. "I may not have told you the whole truth."

"Why would you keep information from me? Aren't I a member of your party?" Realization crosses his face. "It's because you don't trust me."

Valindra faces him. "I don't trust you entirely. When we found you, you told us that you had been an acquaintance of Chrom's, and you were so kind to inform us that he was the head of this operation. Serena knew that you were arrested five years ago. And you knew that we were headed towards the library. How did you know that it was the library?"

He hesitates to answer. "I was here five years ago." Three's beak drops open as he stares at Leucious. Serena glares. Valindra cocks an eyebrow at him. "Chrom had me help him clear the family out of here so that he could run his operation. I am not proud of what I did, but I did it for a good reason!"

"What good reason could there be for scaring a family out of their home?" Serena asks him, mad. She knew that Valindra was making an unwise decision to trust him.

"He was threatening to hurt my family." She was surprised, but quickly hid it. Leucious looked truly upset. "I cannot lose the only family members that I have left."

"But you were arrested for smuggling?" Valindra asks him. *His story doesn't seem to be adding up...*

"Chrom found out that I had planned to return a young girl that he was planning to smuggle out of the town. He was going to sell her as a sex slave. He alerted the Watch as to my whereabouts and told them that I was a smuggler. He also planted a gold necklace on my being that he had smuggled from the next town over."

Serena's features soften a little. There were parts that were lining up with the report, but she didn't know about the first part.

"You were framed?" Valindra asks him.

"Yes!" Leucious exclaims. "I was going to report him to the Watch as soon as I had managed to escape from here with the child and the other goods that he plans to- "

"Wait, did you say that there's a child being held hostage here?" Serena interrupts him.

"Yes?"

Serena turns her attention to Valindra. "Valindra, we- "

Valindra interrupts her. "I know. Everyone, move. We have to search the rest of the house and find the child."

They exit the room. Valindra and Leucious each grab a torch. Valindra winces as the pain in her shoulder when she reaches up.

"Partner up. We light the rest of the torches and finish investigating up here before we move downstairs."

She walks up, Three hurrying to follow her. Serena looks at Leucious.

"I guess we're partnered up again."

"Are you sure that you want to partner with me? You don't even trust me." He accuses her.

She places a hand on his shoulder. She takes a big breath. "You gave us some information that we needed. And I believe your story."

She pries the torch from him gently and walks away. He follows her.

They turn the corner before he speaks again. "Why do you believe my story?"

They stop. Leucious hands her an unlit torch and she ignites it.

"I did some research on you when you were arrested. You were a doctor that helped others regardless of their status." Leucious places the lit torch back in the wall sconce. "And that's something that I admired about you." She admits.

Leucious looks at her and sees that her face has reddened. "Really?" She nods.

They continue walking down the hall, lighting the torches as they go. Eventually, Leucious takes the torch from her. Finally, they come to another set of doors.

"Then you know that I lost my medical license. That's how I became an associate of Chrom's. He offered to help me, and I was foolish enough to accept it."

"I'm sorry to hear that."

"You have no need to apologize. Besides," he turns his head and smiles at her, "I'm a changed man."

Her blush darkens. His smile forms into a smirk at her reaction. He turns his attention to the doors and opens them.

When they walk in, they find the scene to be worse than the previous room. The bed has been flipped over; blankets crumpled in piles on the floor. Fewer books and papers lay scattered on the floor. Most of the books are still in the bookcases, laying on their sides. A window is shattered.

"I do wonder what Chrom was looking for." Leucious wonders aloud.

Serena walks along the length of the wall, looking around. "I have the faintest idea. It seems to be this way in all of the rooms." She comes across a broken door. "Even the closet has been ransacked. Looks like there might be some cloth missing…"

Three's voice comes from outside the room. "Hey guys, look at what we found!"

He hops in, jewels and necklaces in his arms. He finds a clear spot on the floor and lays everything down, spreading them out so that they don't overlap each other. Valindra walks through the doorway just as Serena and Leucious gather around Three.

"Where did you find these?" Serena asks. She investigates the pile; rubies, sapphires, and emeralds are mixed in with the gold and diamond jewelry.

"There were lots of chests in the room that Val-mom and I investigated."

Valindra leans against the doorway. "Taking the other items into consideration, I would say that it was the servant's quarters."

Leucious is confused. "If you're just coming from the servant's quarters, then why did they have these?"

"They were probably stealing from the family." Serena says.

"I'm surprised that Chrom didn't find these."

"The door was locked." Valindra explains. "Three picked it. I don't know why Chrom didn't just break the door down or used his axe." Three starts to put the jewels in his pack, glee on his face. "Just remember that we are returning those to the family."

Three looks at her, pouting. "Do we have to?"

"Yes, Three, we do. But you can hold onto them until then."

Three perks up again as he starts to pack them away again. Valindra looks at Serena and Leucious.

"Did you find anything in here?"

"The usual mess." Leucious answers.

"It looks like there might be some cloth missing from the closet." Serena answers.

Valindra shrugs and quirks an eyebrow. "Remember that we are dealing with smugglers." They nod, agreeing with her statement. "Well, if that's everything, I think that we should finish with the downstairs level next."

They all mutter in agreement. They walk out of the room, Leucious leaving last. They start making their way to the staircase.

"Hey, does anyone know what time it is?" Leucious asks. "I'm starting to feel hungry."

Three goes to stand in the sunlight filtering through the hole in the ceiling. He looks up, searching for something.

"Uh, I'd say about 9:30am."

"Ah, good." Leucious rubs his hands together. "Who's up for some breakfast?"

Chapter 7

Of Riddles and Ravens

$\mathscr{L}$eucious and Serena are waiting in the main foyer, torch still in

hand. Three waits at the bottom of the stairs, arms outstretched towards

the top. Valindra steps off the last step, holding onto the banister.

"I'm fine, Three. I'm in no need of assistance."

"Oh, gee, Val-mom, I'm just worried about you."

"If I can survive going against an ancient red dragon, then I can

survive a bite from a wild pandimensional beast."

Three shrugs. "Okay then, Val-mom."

Three hops off in the direction of the three hallways. Valindra joins

Serena and Leucious in the foyer. Serena gives her a look of shock.

"You survived an ancient red dragon? That's a story I want to hear

later."

Valindra rolls her left shoulder. "I lied." She whispered. "I've never

faced an ancient red dragon."

"Why would you say that then?" Leucious asks, his voice almost

lowered to a whisper.

"So that he would stop worrying about me." Valindra whispers. Her expression softens, as if she were sad. "It's dangerous to worry about a party member when we have yet to investigate the rest of the building."

"A very pretty thing I am, fluttering in the pale-blue sky." Three singsongs. They look at him as he waits for them in the middle of the three hallways. "Delicate, fragile on the wing, indeed I am a pretty thing."

"What are you going on about?" Serena asks him, wondering if he's gone mad.

He looks at them. "It's a riddle. I love riddles. Can you figure it out?"

Leucious looks pensive. Serena is obviously confused. Why would he spout a riddle right now? Valindra shakes her head, not knowing the answer.

"I'm sorry, Three. I've never heard that one before." She tells him.

He shrugs. "That's okay. Let me know when you figure it out. So, shouldn't we be going?"

"Yes, we should. Leucious, be ready with the torch."

As if breaking free from a spell, Leucious shakes his head. He nods, heading for the last unexplored hallway. The girls follow along. Once regrouped, they start walking down the left side of the hall. They shortly come upon a door with a torch above it. Leucious lights the torch as Three opens the door.

Sunlight peers in through the window. A long wooden table sits in the middle of the room, chairs pushed in around it. A cabinet sits in the corner, plates on display. A two-tiered cart sits against the opposite wall.

"Dining room." Three tells the party.

They continue down the hall, shortly coming upon another door. Leucious once again lights the torch above it. Three opens the door.

A smaller table sits in this room with fewer chairs around it. There is a smaller, nondescript cabinet against the wall. But nothing else of interest.

"Another dining room." Three says.

Valindra looks in through the doorway. "Must have been where the servants ate."

They move across the hall to the next door, this one with a torch on either side of the door. Leucious lights them. Serena opens the door and walks in.

"A third dining room. But this one's been used recently."

The others join her. This dining room is the largest, with a longer table and more chairs. Natural light fills the room from the floor to ceiling windows. There are more cabinets in here, displaying lots of ornate plates, bowls, and teacups. Serena stands at the head of the table, closest to them. Dirty plates and half-empty cups sit on the table.

"This room must have been used for dinner parties. The first one was probably just for the family or informal dinners." Serena says.

"Looks like Chrom's men just broke their fast." Leucious says, eyeing the plates and cups. His stomach growls. "God, I'm so hungry."

Serena throws an apple towards him. Valindra catches it before it can hit him in the face. She hands it to him. He gladly accepts, taking a bite from it.

"How often do they feed the hostages?" Valindra asks him.

"Not often." Leucious answers her around a mouthful of apple. "Maybe once every three or four days."

She nods. She ponders over when the boy would have last eaten. "We arrived here yesterday. The Cliffbane boy left home the night before that, so we can assume that he ate that night. He probably arrived here yesterday morning."

"This would be his second day without food." Serena states, following Valindra's thought. "Leucious, how many hostages are there?"

He swallows. "The kid and I were the only ones left. Chrom had the others killed then thrown into the ocean after they tried to riot."

That did not bode well for the child.

"We should go. His safety relies on us." Valindra walks out of the room.

Serena is the last to leave the dining room, closing the door behind her. They walk down the rest of the hallway, entering the kitchen. Leucious walks up to the back wall and lights a couple of torches. He goes left, lighting more torches as he comes up to them. Valindra goes right, then rejoins Serena and Three.

"Nothing but pots and pans."

"Hey, guys?" Leucious calls.

The party goes left. Leucious stands at the very corner of the room. He looks at them and points at the wall.

"Found the door to the basement."

....

Three stands in front of the door. The rest of the party surrounds him. He attempts to pick the lock, getting more frustrated with each passing second. Finally, he sighs before removing his lockpicking tools from the door.

"I can't pick the lock." He says, discouraged.

Valindra lightly pats his shoulder. "That's okay, Three. We'll find another way to unlock the door."

"We could try the writing on the door." Serena says.

Three lets out a caw, jumping back with a start. They look at the door. Gold letters shine on the door in a weird script, the rune for ice above them.

Leucious inspects it closely. "What language is that?"

Serena scoffs. "Don't tell me you can't read Dwarven." The rest of the party remains silent. Serena sighs, rubbing her hand against her head. "It looks to be a riddle."

"Ou, I love riddles!" Three exclaims, excitedly. "What does it say?"

Serena lowers her hand and looks at the door. "It reads: 'Power enough to smash ships and crush roofs. Yet still it must fear the sun. What is it?'"

"That's easy! It's ice!"

The words disappear after Three answers, a lock clicking. Valindra tries the doorhandle and pulls. The door creaks open. Torches light the descending stairwell. Leucious sets his torch in an empty sconce. Serena raises her shield and draws her sword before heading down the stairs in the lead. Three follows, then Leucious and then Valindra, who closes the door.

A low growl resonates up the stairwell. Serena stops and stares ahead.

"What is it?" Valindra asks, whispering.

She doesn't answer. Instead, she hurries down the rest of the stairs. The party hurries after her. As they near the bottom, they see a wererat scratching at a hastily made barricade.

"What in the name of Kodkod is that?" Three asks.

The wererat turns and looks at them. It snarls.

Leucious is quick to act, quickly casting. The blue-white beam hits the wererat square in the chest. It growls and snarls some more, barring its teeth.

Serena moves towards the wererat and strikes, but the creature seems unaffected by it.

"Shit! Does anyone have a silvered weapon?" She asks.

The wererat bites at Serena, but she brings her shield up in time for it to bounce off the shield.

Valindra moves closer, her rapier drawn. "I do not. What about you, Three?"

"Nope."

"Then stay out of harm's way!" Valindra tells him.

"No way! I'll help keep it busy!" Three is adamant about this, moving to circle behind the wererat.

"Here goes nothing!" Leucious casts again.

Two blue-white beams shoot from Leucious's hands. They hit the wererat. It snarls louder, stumbling back a little from the force of the beams.

Serena attacks again, but the creature looks fine after her attack. The wererat retaliates against her, which she blocks again.

"Don't you have any other spells?" She asks Leucious, peeved that she can only distract the enemy.

Valindra pierces the wererat with her rapier, but it looks unfazed. It turns its head towards her.

Valindra can only smirk. Her blade glows red-hot, smoke and the smell of burning fur coming from the wererat.

It squeaks in rage and pain as it ignites. It stumbles away from her blade. Three moves back, to not catch on fire.

Leucious frantically flips through his spell book. "Uh..." he stretches his hand out towards the wererat, hoping that this would be enough to work. "Magic Missile."

Three darts emit from his hand and hit the wererat. It starts to whimper and pant. It takes a staggering step forward. Serena steps back as it tumbles to the ground in a pile of ashes. The fire dies down quickly.

"That was fun." Valindra says, sarcastically.

"You! What did you do to Chrom?"

The voice comes from behind the barricade. They look and see a human male, tanned skin, dark shaggy hair, and a beard, pointing at them, a sword in his other hand. Leucious's complexion turns ashen. A few other people behind the man are brandishing swords.

Serena starts to freak out. *Crap! What do we say?*

"He is dead." She looks at Valindra. How can she be calm in this situation? "Us three killed him. Leucious had nothing to do with Chrom's death."

"Are you trying to get us killed?!" Serena exclaims.

"He's dead?" The man lowers his sword. Valindra nods, confirming what she said. He starts to chuckle. "Thank god. Thank you! You've freed us all!"

Serena is surprised at his response. "Wait, what?"

"Chrom threatened our lives if we didn't work for him. He would find us at our lowest and offer to help us. The threats came along if we tried to get out of his operation."

"That's terrible." Three says.

"It is, mate." He answers Three. "Who among you is the leader?"

Valindra claps Serena's shoulder. "Serena here is our leader."

"What are you doing?" Serena whisper-yells to her.

"Trust me." Valindra whispers back, calmly. "You're a human like them. They are bound to trust you more. Besides, this is your case." She points out.

The henchman moves a few items from the barricade, breaking it down. Once there is a big enough path cleared, he walks over to Serena, his right hand extended.

"The name's Johnathan. I see that you're a member of the town's Watch."

Serena extends her own hand, shaking his. "It is nice to make your acquaintance, Johnathan. And yes. I am a member of the Watch."

Johnathan is enthusiastic when shaking her hand. "We will happily confess to our crimes and report Chrom."

"I'm sure that my party and I would be able to clear your names."

Johnathan's expression changes as he looks at Leucious. "Would you do that?" He asks him. "Chrom never threatened your life."

"Because he knew that I wouldn't care if he threatened my life. He threatened my family instead. And framed me for smuggling that girl five years ago, as well as a necklace from the next town over. I will be happy once our names have been cleared." Leucious informs him.

Johnathan returns his attention to Serena. "If you and your party will do that, then we're going to need a new captain. Will you be our captain, Serena?"

Serena's eyes widen.

"Say yes." Valindra whispers, loud enough for only her to hear.

Is she crazy? Serena thinks to herself. "Yes. I will be your captain."

"Great. Come outback, meet the rest of the crew."

He walks past the barricade, the other crew members that hid behind it with him following behind. Serena waits until they're out of sight before slapping Valindra across the face. Three squawks at her actions.

"Are you insane? Why did you get me to agree to be their new captain?"

Valindra rubs her cheek. "Because then you can get used to commanding a group."

"But to start out with commanding an entire ship? You're better suited than I to be captain."

"You will become accustomed to it. Now, captain, lead the way."

Serena leads the way all right, fuming the entire way. Once the party meets up with the ship's crew in the back room, all eyes turn to them. Johnathan stands beside Serena.

"Well, lads, the news on Chrom is that he's dead." Johnathan tells them.

The crew shouts in excitement. Johnathan waits until they quiet down.

"Meet our new captain, Serena." He introduces her.

Another henchman speaks up. "A woman captain?" They look at him, his red hair also shaggy. "That's rare. Welcome aboard." He holds up a mug.

"Thank you." Serena says.

"What would you have us do first, captain?" Johnathan asks.

Serena plays with her hands, nervous. "Well, uh… first I would like to resign as captain."

Valindra stands straighter, her eyes narrowing as she looks at Serena. *What is she doing? Is she mad?* Valindra thinks.

"… and I would like to appoint my companion, Valindra Theharice, as your new captain."

Just as I thought. She is mad. Valindra answers her own questions.

Johnathan doesn't look bothered. "Okay. So, captain, what should we do first?"

"Tell me first: Do any of you have specific roles aboard the ship?" She asks.

"No. We all help out wherever it's needed." Johnathan informs her.

"Do you have a treasurer?"

"No. Chrom took care of all of that himself." Johnathan explains. "Said he didn't trust any of us to look after it."

She nods. Three pulls on her cape. She crouches.

"Ask if the ship has a crow's nest." Three requests, his voice lowered.

"Yes, Three." She asks Johnathan: "Does the ship have a crow's nest?"

"It used to have one. It came crashing down in a terrible storm last year. Chrom decided not to fix it."

Three looks disappointed. Valindra pats and smooths the feathers on his head.

"Are you currently holding any hostages?" Valindra asks him, deciding that it would be best to ask in case something had gone wrong.

"A boy. I can fetch him if you'd like."

"Please do, Johnathan."

Johnathan walks off, soon disappearing around the corner. Valindra stands, looking out over her new crew. The second henchman, still unnamed, speaks up.

"Will you be giving us new roles, captain?"

She thinks for a moment before answering. "Not if you don't want them. And, if you wish to, you're free to abandon ship and return home to your families."

There is a quiet murmur amongst them, before a third henchman speaks up.

"All of our families died from the plague six years ago. We're our own family now."

"I'm sorry about your families. But I am glad that you're staying aboard."

A few more minutes pass by. Three interacts with the crew, wanting to get to know them. Leucious decides to sit with the second henchman, hoping to explain his situation. He's offered some bread as he sits, and he gladly takes it.

"Let go of me!" A young voice cries from around the corner.

Valindra and Serena look towards the sound of the voice. Johnathan rounds the corner with the Cliffbane boy, nearly dragging him by the upper arm. He's struggling to get away from Johnathan. He soon stands in front of Valindra, chains around his wrists and ankles. She crouches down to his height, needing to look up slightly. She notices that there are rope burns around his wrists.

She speaks in a soft voice, one so soft that Serena is surprised that she can muster a tone like it. "What's your name, sweetheart?"

"Why do you care?"

"Because I would like to know." He remains silent. "We won't hurt you. Your mother sent us to look for you."

"What about those guys? They hurt me earlier."

"They were being ordered by an awfully bad man earlier. But they work for me now. They won't hurt you anymore."

He looks at her, trying to decipher whether she's telling him the truth. He finally tells her: "Thadeus."

She smiles, also soft. "Hello, Thadeus. My name is Valindra, but you can call me Val if you'd like." She opens her pack and pulls out an apple. She holds it out for him. "Here, eat this. You must be hungry."

Thadeus reluctantly takes the apple from Valindra. He takes a bite from it.

Right now, it was just the two of them. She was creating a space safe enough for him. "Can you tell me why you came back here?"

He swallows another bite of apple. "I came back for Bunny."

"Your stuffed rabbit?" He nods, taking another bite. "Why were you coming back for him after all this time?"

"My father wouldn't let me." He tells her around a mouthful of apple. "And then he died last winter. I brought his sword with me so that I could protect myself."

She nods, understanding. "Johnathan, get these chains off of him."

Johnathan follows her order, crouching beside Thadeus to remove his restraints. Without her giving another order, another crewmate retrieves a steel sword with an ornate hilt from a crate along the east wall. He returns it to Thadeus.

"Thank you, all of you. But I still need to find Bunny."

"About that…" Valindra waves Three over.

Three walks over, taking his pack off as he makes his way over. Once he reaches them, he opens his pack and reaches in, pulling out the stuffed rabbit.

"Here you go." He holds Bunny out to Thadeus.

"Bunny!" Thadeus exclaims, excited. He takes Bunny from Three and hugs it to him tightly. "Where did you find him?"

"He was sitting on your bed. He's got some dried mud in his fur." He gives a low caw as he points to the mud.

"Thank you, um…"

"Three." Valindra looks at him. "Oh, you're welcome."

Serena taps Valindra on the shoulder. "Valindra, we should probably get him home."

"You're right." She stands and looks out amongst her new crew. "Us four are going to take young Thadeus back to his mother. We'll meet you at the Watch station to verify your stories."

"We'll see you there, captain. Safe travels." Johnathan wishes her.

"And you."

She leads Thadeus out by the hand, Serena and Three following behind. Leucious stays seated with the rest of the crew. Three comes back and looks at him.

"Aren't you coming, Leucious? Or do I have to invite you?"

……………..

Leucious stands at the door of the current Cliffbane residence, his tail swinging nervously. He holds a few papers in his hands. Thadeus, hugging Bunny, stands beside him. The rest of the party waits on the other side of the fence, sitting on their horses. Valindra holds the rope around the mare, Three sitting behind her.

"Are you sure that it was a good idea to let him go up there alone?" Serena asks Valindra, nervously waiting for the outcome.

"You haven't questioned any of my actions yet."

Misses Cliffbane opens the door. When she sees her son, she welcomes him into her arms, crying. A few seconds pass by before they see Leucious turn and point towards them. She looks past him, towards the three of them. They all wave, and she waves back, a smile on her tear-striped face. Leucious turns back and continues talking with Misses Cliffbane. She suddenly disappears into the house.

"What is she doing?" Serena asks aloud.

They can see a pouch in her hands when she comes back out. She hands it to Leucious, who tries to give it back. She refuses. Leucious slouches in defeat, then stands straight, rubbing the back of his neck. He says his goodbyes, then walks back to the party.

"What did she hand to you?" Valindra asks him as he approaches.

He sighs. "A pouch containing four-thousand gold coins. And she said that Three can keep the jewels that he found."

Three pokes his head out around Valindra's side, perky. "Really? Thank you!" He yells the last part towards the house.

"Very good, Three. Leucious, why don't you hold onto the gold? We still have to return to the Watch, and I have horses to return."

"Are you sure that you want me holding onto the gold? I thought you didn't trust me."

"I was wrong to not trust you. You proved just how trustworthy you are. I apologize for ever doubting you."

"I accept your apology."

He mounts the mare, taking the makeshift reins from Valindra. He and Serena take off towards town. Valindra and Three are about to take off when Thadeus calls out to them.

"Val! Thanks for saving me! And thank you for making it possible for mother and me to go back home!"

"You're welcome! Don't be afraid to send a bird if you need help moving!" She yells up to them.

"We will!" Misses Cliffbane yells back. "Safe travels, adventurers! Thank you for bringing my boy home!"

Valindra and Three smile before she steers Cider and gallops off, starting to catch up to Serena and Leucious.

Chapter 8

Orianna Weary

*I*t is dusk in the town of Kilmarnock when they reach the Watch headquarters. The party made their way inside, greeting the other guards and the ship's crew. The guards congratulate Serena on solving the mystery surrounding Cliffbane Manor.

A door opens, and an older man stands in the doorway. His brown hair is streaked with grey, some white patches in his mustache. The wrinkles around his brown eyes become more defined as he narrows his eyes at Serena.

"You." He points at her. "My office. Now." He walks back into the room, leaving the door open.

"Oh, no." Serena gulps. "I'm in trouble." Her voice showed how scared she was.

"It can't be that bad, Serena." Three tries to cheer her up. "We'll be rooting for you out here!"

"Bring your friends in with you." The older man calls from his office.

"Now we're all in trouble." Valindra states.

The other guards chuckle, but a quick glance from Leucious shuts them up. The four of them make their way into the office.

....

"What is the meaning of this?" He asks the group after the door is closed.

"Please, let me explain – "

He cuts Serena off. "No, you're going to listen. You took off with this job posting, knowing damn well that you don't have the skill nor the experience to handle it."

"I think we handled it pretty well." Three says.

The older man only glares at Three. "Shut up, bird. I'm not talking to you."

Three's eyes widen, hurt. He cuddles into Valindra's side, who wraps her arms around him, comforting him.

"You should never speak to a child like that." She says, glaring at him.

"Unless you have a child, I would watch my tongue about how to speak to a child."

"That's enough, father." Serena says, pissed at him.

His eyes widen only a little, surprised that Serena would speak to him like that. "Excuse me?" He raises an eyebrow at her. "What did you just say to me?"

She starts to cower. That gaze has been thrown at her one too many times, especially since she joined the Watch.

"She said that's enough." Leucious stands in front of her. She is surprised to see him putting himself between her and her father.

Her father glowers. "Creed."

"Sir."

"You better have been staying out of trouble. Because I would love to throw you back in prison."

"As much as I know you would love that, sir, I am saddened to say that I have been on my best behaviour."

"It's true, father." His attention is returned to Serena. The others look at her. "He helped us bring the Cliffbane boy home. He helped us get out of there alive."

"He's a criminal, Serena!"

"A wrongly accused one!" She argues back.

He scoffs. "You don't know what you're talking about."

She moves around Leucious, placing her hands against her father's desk and leans towards him. Not trying to threaten him but trying to plead with him.

"I've read his file, sir. He was imprisoned for smuggling a young girl and stealing jewellery from the next town over."

Her father leans back in his chair. "I know that, Serena. I wrote the report myself."

"What you don't know is that the one who put in the anonymous is the one who actually committed those crimes."

He rolls his eyes. "No, he didn't. He was an innocent man worried about the girl."

"Have you seen him around town since he put in the tip?" She asks him. "Or the girl?"

"Well, no, but we returned the girl to her family."

"Sir, if I may." Valindra speaks up. They look at her. She's still comforting a crying Three. "If the crime was reported five years ago, who's to say that the girl wasn't kidnapped again?"

"It is possible that Chrom went back for her." Leucious states, his hand rubbing his chin. "He was pretty adamant about selling her."

"Regardless of whether that is true, the Tiefling is a criminal. As well as those pirates out there. They should all be arrested." Captain Stoutbrow states.

"No, father." Serena argues.

"You want those criminals to walk free?"

"There is a good reason, sir." She tells him.

"And what is that, Serena? What 'good reason' is there to let them walk free?" He uses air quotations, questioning her statement. He leans his elbows against his oak desk, clasping his hands together in front of his face.

Oh boy, I am going to be in more trouble than I bargained for. Serena thinks.

"Their lives were threatened." She says.

"You're only repeating what you were told. Don't be so naïve." He dismisses her remark.

Serena breathes in deeply through her nose. Three leaves Valindra's grasp and bumps his head against Serena's arm. The tension in the room is high. Leucious clears his throat.

"If I may, sir?" He asks.

The captain of the guard looks at him sternly. "Speak quickly, Creed."

"As you know, I was arrested and imprisoned for smuggling five years ago. I served my sentence and was in good behaviour the entire time." Captain Stoutbrow nods, telling him to go on. "That crew out there are who I served with before I was arrested. We were all good people. Chrom had threatened their lives because he knew that they had no family."

"Did he threaten you, too? Or were you his right-hand man?"

"I was the only member of the crew with a family. He threatened them instead of me."

The captain of the Watch was silent for a moment. "How can I know that you're not lying?"

"The crew wouldn't have volunteered to confess to what they had done if Chrom were still alive." Valindra says.

He narrows his eyes even more at Valindra. "What do you mean if he were still alive? Are you confessing to a murder, miss…?"

"Theharice."

"Miss Theharice. Because murder is a crime."

She shrugs. "I've probably done worse in your eyes than murder." Three looks at her, excited at the possibility that maybe Val-mom wasn't such a goody-two-shoes. "But if you head up to the manor, you'll see for yourself. Just know, he was killed in order to save not only Thadeus Cliffbane, but Leucious and your daughter as well."

He grinds his teeth.

I seem to have hit a nerve. Valindra thinks. *Maybe if I hit the right one, he'll let up on my party…*

"If we hadn't done what we did, then your daughter would have ended up either dead, or sold off to someone to do with her as they pleased. That crew out there, my crew, wouldn't have helped us bring Thadeus home and want to repent for their sins if they were truly ill-natured."

Ah, there's the holy woman. Serena thought after Valindra mentioned the crew repenting their sins.

"Your crew?" Her father asks. "Any rogue that has a ship crew could be up to no good."

Serena whips her head around to her father, ready to defend her friend. "She is a paladin." Her father looks at her. "She dresses like a rogue because it is easier to move. And her crew told us that before anyone became their new captain, they would confess to what they've done. They've kept true to their word. As far as I'm concerned, they've upheld their end of the law by confessing." She stands straighter and crosses her arms.

"How can we be sure that they won't continue smuggling if they walk free?"

"We'll work for you." Valindra suggests.

Everyone looks at her at that statement. Captain Stoutbrow motions for her to keep talking.

"Any special quests that you have, we will do. Especially those that require overseas travel."

He seems to consider this for a moment. "No. You can't be trusted to run off."

"I'll go with them."

"No. Absolutely not, Serena." He denies immediately.

"It is my decision, father. This way, there will be an official member of the Watch on board the ship." She squares her shoulders and stares at her father. "You cannot change my mind."

He breathes deeply before sighing. He brings his head to rest against the palm of his hand. He knew from raising Serena that she wasn't going to back down without being forcefully restrained. Arguing with her wouldn't help, either; she seemed to have inherited his attitude.

"Your crew should be able to leave here in a week. We must conduct our search and reclaim all stolen and smuggled items. And, as a thank you for the completion of this quest, there is a pay of five-hundred gold coins for each of you. Claim it at the front desk."

They all nod and turn to leave. Leucious holds the door for the rest of them and was about to leave when the captain called him.

"Stay out of trouble, Creed. You were able to escape sentencing this time."

He nods before leaving.

Serena makes her way towards the front desk, waiting as the clerk retrieves their pay. Leucious, Three, and Valindra join the crew.

"How did it go in there?" Johnathan asked once they were close enough.

"Messy. But, without going into too much detail, you should all be free to walk within the week." Valindra informs her crew. They cheer in celebration. She waits for the noise to subside. "Johnathan, what is the name of the ship? And where is it located?"

"She's 'The Infernal Jackdaw', Captain. She's docked at the shoreline by the manor."

"Thank you, Johnathan." She addresses the rest of the crew. "Attention, crew of 'The Infernal Jackdaw'." They all look to her. "I would like to be prepared for take off when we receive our next quest. That means that we prepare to set sail when you leave here. That is all."

Johnathan and the rest of the crew give her an "Aye-aye, captain!" before they leave to shop for supplies.

She sighs, taking in a big breath. Three puffs out his chest, drying the last stray tear with his arm. Leucious offers him a handkerchief, but Three refuses it. Leucious pockets the cloth just as Serena approaches them, four pouches in hand.

"Here we are; one pouch each. What should we do now?" Serena asks, handing the others their pouches of gold.

"I don't know about anyone else, but I'm getting food. And something to drink." Leucious states. "Anyone care to join?"

"Supper would be nice." Serena agrees, her stomach starting to growl.

Valindra nods in agreement. Three pulls repeatedly on her cloak.

"Hey, Val-mom, shouldn't we be taking the horses back?"

"Yes, we should. Come along, Three." They make their way towards the door before she looks back at the other two. "Meet you at the tavern?"

……………..

A man walks through the door of the Iron Lamp Tavern. It is busier than usual, most patrons flocking around a table. He spots an empty seat at the bar and sits at it.

"Just an ale, Torren."

Torren leaves the bar to fetch the man's order.

"Rough day?" The man sitting to his right asks.

"Just another bloody Monday." He sighs. "Worst day of the week."

"Oh no, you've got it all wrong." A feather-light voice tells him. They look towards the source of the voice. "Tuesdays are the worst day of the week." The red-skinned Tiefling states.

"What are you going on about, woman? Everyone knows that Mondays are the worst."

A cinnamon-coloured pseudodragon peeps its head outside of her cloak hood, a strand of white-blue hair laying across its head.

"Mondays are one of the better days of the week." She tells him. She brings a hand up to scratch at the pseudodragon's chin. "It's not the best, but it beats Tuesday. Wednesdays are okay, and Thursdays are the best. Fridays aren't always the greatest, but still better than Tuesdays, and moods shift between Saturday and Sunday, depending on what happens on those days."

"That is the maddest thing I've ever heard. Where the bloody hell are you from?" The man asks her.

She picks up her mug, smirking. "Hell." She takes a drink.

....

It is nearly nightfall when Three and Valindra finish returning the horses, on their way to the tavern. Three hops alongside Valindra, not having any issue keeping pace with her.

"It was nice of Cain to only make you pay for one day for taking Cider."

She gives Three a small smile. "He was very grateful to have his mare returned. I wasn't expecting this discount after we had already come to an agreement."

"Me neither." Three chirps. "And he was so nice to offer his services in the future!"

"He was. It is always a good idea to have alliances within a town."

A grey-brown moth crosses their path. Three hops after it, chasing it. Valindra stops to watch, her smile getting wider, watching Three play. She thinks back to his riddle, an idea crossing her thoughts.

"Three?"

He stops chasing after the moth and looks at her. "Yeah, Val-mom?"

"The answer to your riddle. Is it a butterfly?"

He smiles at her. He hops back over to her, enveloping her in a big hug. "I knew you would get it!"

They break the hug, continuing their way to the tavern. The lights are lit by the lanterns, making it easy to see. They spot Leucious and Serena standing outside of the tavern, seeming to be in conversation. Valindra didn't know if it was a trick of the light or not, but it looked like Serena was blushing.

Leucious was about to open the door when Three cawed, getting their attention. He and Serena turn towards them, waving when they see them.

As Valindra and Three get closer to the tavern, they can hear fighting coming from inside.

"We thought that you two were already indoors." Serena says.

"It should now be apparent that we aren't. Any idea what started the fighting?" Valindra asks.

"No. We just got here ourselves." Leucious states.

The door opens a crack. Three stands in the doorway, the sounds from inside becoming louder. He's about to push it open the rest of the way before he turns to the party.

"Well, what are you three waiting for? An invitation?"

....

They stand in the tavern, keeping close to the door. Valindra has her hand placed firmly on Three's shoulder, keeping him close to her and away from the raucous. The tavern's patrons are fighting amongst themselves.

"What the hell happened here?" Serena asks, astounded at the scene in front of her.

"That's a good question. But aren't taverns usually like this?" Leucious asks, seeing as he hasn't been in a tavern in a few years.

There is a chirp at the sound of his voice, and this cinnamon-coloured object goes skittering across the floor, avoiding people's feet and ignoring those fighting on the floor.

"What's that crawling on the floor?" Three pipes up, seeing it more easily than the others.

The rest of them narrow their eyes, squinting as they try to make out the shape of the crawling creature. It gets closer and closer to them with every passing second.

"Is that?... There's no way… Firefly?" Leucious speaks. Firefly appears at his feet. He picks up the small cat-sized dragon, who rubs up against Leucious's face. "If you're here, then…" He investigates the fighting crowd. "Orianna?"

The fighting pauses when he yells, all eyes turning towards the party. The female Tiefling, Orianna, is pinning a guy to the floor.

She gasps, then squeals. "Leuci!"

"What are you doing?"

The rest of the party is confused. There were two Tieflings in town?

"This man was saying that Mondays are the worst day of the week. And I said that Tuesdays are actually the worst day."

"Tuesdays are the worst." Leucious agrees. "But he's human, they think differently. Why are you pinning that one to the ground?"

The other three grow more visibly confused.

Orianna smiles, elongated fangs prominent in her smile. "I may or may not have started a bar fight."

Leucious pinches the bridge of his nose with his unoccupied hand. He sighs. "Of course you did. Please don't mind her, everyone. In fact, next round is on me!"

Everyone in the tavern cheers. They help each other off the floor and pick up the overturned tables and chairs.

Leucious makes his way over to Orianna, the party following him. Orianna gets off the human male and stands, making her way to Leucious. She throws her arms around his shoulders when he gets close enough.

Who the hell is this woman? Was the thought going through the party's minds.

"It is so good to hug you again. When did you get out of prison?"

"It's a rather long story." He explains. He lets go of her, keeping a hand on her shoulder. "I'll give you the shorter version over a meal and a drink. Would you like to join us?"

"Us?"

"My companions and I." He gestures, still holding Firefly, at the party. "They saved my life."

"Who're you?" Three asks, staring at her goat-like horns.

"Orianna, this is Three, Val, and Serena. Everyone, this is Orianna." Leucious introduces them. "She's my sister."

"You have a sister?!" All three unanimously exclaim.

....

They sit around a table, food in front of them all and each with a drink in hand. Leucious had just finished telling his sister the events leading up to before they showed up at the tavern.

142

"So, you were let out a couple months ago?" Orianna asks him.

"Yes." Orianna punches his upper arm. "Ow!" He rubs at the spot. "What was that for? That kind of hurt!"

"You should have come see me when you first got out!"

"I was attempting to do that! Chrom must have heard that I was being freed, because his men attacked me as I was on the way to ask about ticket prices. I just told you all of this!"

Valindra leans over to Serena as Leucious and Orianna continue to bicker.

"Do siblings always hit each other?" She whispers.

"It might be normal for some families. My brother and I never hit each other unless we were training.

Orianna gives a small laugh, holding a small piece of her steak up to her animal companion, who happily accepts the meat. "I'm sorry for hitting you, brother."

"I guess you had the right to. How are you? How is Criella?" He asks.

Three has mashed potato all over his beak when he turns his attention away from his food. "Is Criella your other sister?"

"You could say that." Leucious says, taking a drink.

"Criella is my wife." Valindra's and Serena's eyes widen in questioning awe as Orianna explained who the other woman was. "And we're doing great. We moved into another town recently because she got a job as a teacher. She teaches kids how to write and teaches other, younger sorcerers." She explains to the others at the table. "And we volunteer at the library. Or, really, I do when I'm home."

"Still adventuring? What about the house?" Leucious asks.

"We still have the farm. We return there during the summer. And yes, I have been adventuring. I think, however that this was my last adventure. I am retiring."

"If I may ask, why are you retiring? Adventuring is fun." Valindra asks, putting down her fork. This was more interesting to her than her dinner.

Orianna smiles and chuckles. "I'm retiring because I miss my wife. And because she's afraid of me never coming home."

"Why wouldn't you go home?" Three asks.

Serena throws a couple of napkins in his direction. Three picks them up and holds them, more interested in the red-skinned woman sitting beside him.

"You do know the dangers of being an adventurer, right?" Orianna asks him.

Before Three could answer her, the door to the tavern opens. A guardsman from the Watch walks in. All eyes turn to him.

"I am looking for miss Serena Stoutbrow and one Valindra Theharice. Are they here?"

Serena and Valindra stand from the table, excusing themselves. They make their way to the door and leave, following the guardsman.

Three takes a drink, then wipes his beak with a napkin. "So, if you're Leucious's sister, and you have a wife, then do you both have the same last name as him? That's about all I know about families."

"No. Leucious and I did have the same family name, but I took my wife's family name when we married."

"Why?"

"She is the last one in her family." Orianna explains. "Without going into too much detail, her family sacrificed her for riches, and it backfired on them. I wanted to help preserver her name. And we've been talking about adopting from our local orphanage."

"I'm going to be an uncle?" Orianna nods. He pumps a fist into the air. "I'll drink to that!" To which he does.

Three tilts his head. "What's an orphanage?"

"It's a special place where children without families stay so that they can find other families." Orianna tells him.

"Oh."

Serena sits back down. "Sorry about that, everyone."

"Where's Val-mom?"

"She had to go do something." Serena places five gold coins on the table. "At least she paid for her meal."

"Oh. Okay." Three looks dejected, what with Valindra going somewhere without him.

Leucious sits back in his chair, having finished his second plate of food. "Damn, that was good food. So, why was the guardsman looking for you two?"

"We have a new quest. Valindra will inform us of it when we board the ship."

"There is traveling involved? Where are we going?" He tips back his mug, only to find it empty.

"The town of Arkkukari."

"That's my next destination. Mind if I tag along?" Orianna asks.

Serena shrugs. "You'll have to ask Valindra about that." She takes a drink. "I'm fairly certain, though, that she will have no issue with you accompanying us."

"Splendid." She raises her mug. "To new friends!"

Leucious grabbed a new drink just in time to join in on the cheer. They tap their mugs together. Three was excited for new friends. They all drink.

……………..

Valindra stands outside of a door. She knocks solidly. It opens a few seconds later to a man with salt and pepper hair and a beard to match.

"Hello?"

"Hello, sir. Sorry for disturbing you at this late hour, but I have some questions that I'd like to ask of you."

He steps outside and closes the door behind him. He's surprised when he sees that he's eye-level with her eyes.

"What can I help you with?" He asks her, crossing his arms to help protect against the cool air.

"A friend of mine told me that you are the best carpenter in town. Is this true?"

"Yes. I started learning the trade at a young age from my father, and his father before him. Anything you need built; I'll build it for you."

"Excellent. And you're capable of fixing anything I may need repaired?"

"Yes."

"Have you ever fixed anything on board a ship?"

"Can't say that I have."

"Would you like the opportunity to?"

He looks intrigued at her offer. He invites her inside, where they can discuss the offer in further detail.

Epilogue

The quaint town of Arkkukari is silent. Stars dot the sky,
candlelight flickering in and out of windows. The townhouses stand close
together.

But not every house is silent. Up on the hill, just outside the
immediate town, there is one house that is quite lively. Chairs and tables
are tipped over. Picture frames either hang crookedly on the walls or lay
on the floor, broken glass surrounding them. Bloody handprints and
streaks line the walls.

A Tiefling with indigo skin sits on the floor, curled in on herself in a
corner. Her light purple hair covers her face. She rocks back and forth,
grabbing her head in both hands and crying.

"I can't. I can't do it."

A voice echoes in her head. "You can and you will, my child.
Embrace your true power."

She looks across from her, blood streaking from a cut above her black
eyes. Her face lights up as the body in front of her catches on fire.

Meet the Party

Name: Three

Age: Three years

Race: Avishum (pronounced *avis-shum*)

Height: 3'3"

Weight: 80lbs

Eyes: Black

Skin: N/A

Hair: Purple Black

Found as an egg onboard a pirate ship, Three never knew his real family. The crew of the ship took him in, raising him to be one of them: a pirate. However, his crew left him behind when they last docked together, and he's been trying to find a new family ever since. He's smarter than he lets on, but he likes to try to fool others.

Personality Trait: Enjoys sailing to new towns and making new friends over a drink.

Ideals: Aspires to one day own a ship and chart his own destiny.

Bonds: Loyal to his captain first; everyone else comes second.

Flaws: Can't help but pocket loose coins other trinkets that he comes across.

Name: Valindra Theharice

Age: 450 years

Race: Elf (subrace unknown)

Height: 6'0"

Weight: 138lbs

Eyes: Green

Skin: Fair

Hair: Red

A noble by birth, she decided at an early age that she would not watch her people die. She traded the life of a noble woman for that of a knight, putting hard work into training. She fought dragons for centuries, until they were no longer under attack. With this period of calm, Valindra found it difficult to return to the duties that her family assigned to her, so she disappeared in seek of adventure. But she holds another secret, one that she won't tell even on her death bed. Only those close to her know the truth.

Personality Trait: Hurt her, and she will ruin you.

Ideals: Blood runs thicker than water.

Bonds: Her loyalty is unwavering.

Flaws: She secretly thinks that everyone is beneath her.

Name: Serena Stoutbrow

Age: 20 years

Race: Human

Height: 5'5"

Weight: 155lbs

Eyes: Brown

Skin: Sandy

Hair: Brown

Her father never allowed her to do the same things that her brother did when she was younger, but probably for a good reason; her brother, as far as they know, died while on a mission. She decided to step up and show her father that she can help him. She was finally admitted to the Watch, and now she has a lot to prove. She's memorized almost everything she's ever read, and now she's considered a know-it-all, which impresses no one at the Watch. Yes, lots to prove.

Personality Trait: Always polite and respectful.

Ideals: She's very responsible and does what she must to obey authority.

Bonds: She stands up for those who can't stand up for themselves.

Flaws: She will not admit when she's wrong.

Name: Leucious Creed

Age: 33 years

Race: Tiefling

Height: 6′2″

Weight: 210lbs

Eyes: White

Skin: Red

Hair: Black

Leucious always wanted to help people, so he decided to become a doctor. He studied hard and turned out to be pretty good at it. And then everything went to hell when his patients started dying. He lost his license to practice medicine after he discovered that he could bring them back, which caused the town to riot. Chrom found him and offered help, leading him down a wormhole of crime, and eventually to his party.

Personality Trait: Always calm, no matter the situation. He never raises his voice or lets his emotions control him.

Ideals: He's loyal to his friends, not to any ideals; everyone else can take a hike for all he cares.

Bonds: He's guilty of a terrible crime and hopes to redeem himself.

Flaws: Don't tell him what the plan is; he'll either ignore it or forget it.

Name: Orianna Weary (née Creed)

Age: 37 years

Race: Tiefling

Height: 5'11"

Weight: 180lbs

Eyes: White

Skin: Red

Hair: Blue white

Always playing tricks, magic came to her easily, and finding her pact came easier. She met her wife while she was studying at the library. Now, with magic, adventures, and a lovely wife waiting for her, she feels unstoppable. Gods help whoever hurts her family, though; a pissed off Orianna is never good (Leucious knows this very well).

Personality Trait: Pockets anything she thinks is valuable.

Ideals: Determined to make a name for herself.

Bonds: (Unknown at this time).

Flaws: Convinced that no one can fool her the same way that she fools others.